Advance Praise for *Big Cats*

"Each of these pieces is distinguished by Reinhorn['s] [ver]nacular and fresh take on the human condition. Raucous and full of bristling energy."

—*Kirkus Reviews*

"The world of Holiday Reinhorn's fiction is tough and sometimes violent, but her characters are always equal to it, even when they are very young. She is a first-rate writer: original, surprising, and wonderfully honest about America in the troubled twenty-first century."

—Alison Lurie, author of *Imaginary Friends* and *Foreign Affairs*

"In *Big Cats* Holiday Reinhorn unleashes a big, bold, and fully realized talent. Full of wicked wordplay, crackling humor, and sudden menace, the stories in this collection blaze with ambition and originality. Simply put: this is the best new book of short stories I've read in a hell of a long time."

—Brady Udall, author of *The Miracle Life of Edgar Mint*

"Holiday Reinhorn's *Big Cats* is a big ear to every sweet and brutal beat of the human heart. If you want whip-smart stories that have the energy of a rock star, the originality of a mad scientist, and the quiet poetry of your local librarian, grab this book and hold on tight."

—Lisa Lerner, author of *Just Like Beauty*

"Holiday Reinhorn's stories are like nothing you've ever read, though hers are people you have known or seen with familiar lives and grey-scale fates. While offering the idea that we are all haunted, that everyone has a story, Reinhorn is a virtuoso of love and the language it speaks. *Big Cats* is wise, painful, laugh-out-loud funny, and life affirming. Read this book and celebrate a huge new talent."

—Kathleen Hughes, author of *Dear Mrs. Lindbergh*

"Holiday Reinhorn is the kind of writer that gets you laughing just before she knees you in the gut with her powerful prose. With *Big Cats*, Reinhorn shows that she has it all: teeth, claws, bright eyes, a mean strut, and a tender, purring heart."

—Dean Bakopoulos, author of *Please Don't Come Back from the Moon*

"Alcoholics, prima donnas, sinners, and a courier of horse semen—the narrators in *Big Cats* whisper to us from the edges of a smoldering hysteria. *Big Cats* is startling, hilarious, and exhausting."

—Anthony Doerr, author of *About Grace* and *The Shell Collector*

BIG CATS

Stories

HOLIDAY REINHORN

FREE PRESS

New York · London · Toronto · Sydney

FREE PRESS

A Division of Simon & Schuster, Inc.
1230 Avenue of the Americas
New York, NY 10020

FREE PRESS and colophon are trademarks
of Simon & Schuster, Inc.

For information about special discounts for bulk purchases,
please contact Simon & Schuster Special Sales:
1-800-456-6798 or business@simonandschuster.com

DESIGNED BY LAUREN SIMONETTI

Manufactured in the United States of America

10 9 8 7 6 5 4 3 2 1

Library of Congress Cataloging-in-Publication Data
Reinhorn, Holiday.
Big cats: stories / Holiday Reinhorn.
        p.   cm.
1. Pacific Coast (U.S.)—Fiction. I. Title.
      PS3618.E567 B54   2005
      813'.6—dc22   2005040021

ISBN-13: 978-0-7432-7294-0
ISBN-10:   0-7432-7294-3

for Rainn

The lion is the only animal that
allows its captives to return home.

—*Book of Beasts*, 11th century

Contents

CHARLOTTE

The day Mrs. Linkabaugh moved in next door, I cracked my pubic bone in two places. It was 97 degrees, according to the giant thermometer Karl Bongaard had hanging on the side of his house. I was swinging at the time, watching the men from the moving company slide pieces of a fuzzy red water bed out of their truck, when my outgrown swing set pitched like a mechanical bull. A fire hydrant loomed, and I touched down somewhere along the curb. Through a small patch of consciousness, I looked up into the faces of four Mayflower movers as the sky ripped open and all of the clouds dropped to earth like wet rags.

At the Veterans Administration Training Hospital, I was in Room 503 with air-conditioning and a man named Victor Samuels, who pulled open the separating curtain every chance he got and started talking. He said he was originally from St. Louis and that last year his prostate had started hardening up into a little missile. My mother, Bobbie, said we had to be polite to Victor Samuels no matter what because he was probably tortured by the Vietnamese.

Dr. Maryland, the orthopedist, liked Bobbie right away. When he pinned up the X rays and she asked whether smoking was all right if she held it out the window, he said, "Why don't the both of you call me Kevin, okay?"

This kind of thing happens all the time. My father used to say it was because Bobbie could never repulse a man no matter how hard she tried. From the time she was seven to nineteen and a half, my mother, Roberta Marie Peek, was Miss Glendora Heights Southern Division, Miss Teen Hideaway Cove, Miss Young Zuma Beach, Miss Autumn for Sunkist, and third runner-up to Miss La Jolla because she was skinnier then, and nobody could tell she was pregnant.

Even now that she's almost twenty-nine, all the men still like her, and it doesn't matter whether they find out first about the trophies and the train trips and the foot modeling. Jim Juergens, the softball coach from the community center, even came into the girls' locker room when I was changing once and said he had special dreams about making love to Bobbie and getting to be my father. That was the same week Coach Juergens got arrested for walking around the dugout without pants.

Kevin sat in a chair at the foot of my bed and took a long time showing us the X rays.

"As you can see," he said, smiling over at Bobbie, "the fractures are on the left side of the bone. To prevent a limp, I had to actually rebreak the pelvis in the center, just to set the whole thing back in balance."

"This is unbelievable," Bobbie said, leaning over to hand me her last piece of spearmint gum. "I thought this kind of thing only happened to Denny."

Kevin looked at the tan line where Bobbie's wedding ring used to be.

"Who's Denny?" he asked, staring at her like she was the first woman he'd ever seen in his whole life.

Usually, we don't mention Denny to new people right away,

because he has concentration problems and can't keep his hands off things. The last medical bill we had from Denny was when Bobbie took him to the Rub-a-Dub Automatic Car Wash and let him ride through it in the driver's seat all alone. He got into the glove compartment, where Bobbie left her purse, and swallowed three sleeping pills and a half-pack of wintergreen Certs and had to be rushed straight to the Poison Center.

"Denny's my little brother," I said, and Kevin looked relieved. He turned back to the X rays.

"Actually, this was a really easy one," he said to Bobbie, pointing to the problem area in the center of the screen. "Once I had a clean break, I used stainless steel to stitch up the bone."

Bobbie held out her hand and I put the gum wrapper in it.

"Metal stitches," she said, shaking her head at the ceiling. "Holy Christ."

"It's better than a broken leg, though, isn't it?" Kevin said. "At her age, the bones are so soft, it's like sewing tissue. She doesn't even have to wear a cast."

Bobbie sighed into her hands, and Kevin looked like he might cry.

"Please don't worry," he said to her. "The incision will barely leave a scar."

I asked Kevin if he was married.

"Of course he is," Bobbie said, sliding the window shut and brushing her cigarette ashes off the sill. "And whoever guesses how much money Kevin makes in a year gets a free Jell-O."

I guessed a million dollars and Kevin smiled.

"I'm afraid we're only a government hospital around here," he said. "I guess I get the Jell-O."

Later, after Victor Samuels came back from his radiation and went to sleep, Bobbie scooted her chair up next to the bed and told me two things: I had to call my father collect right away to tell him I almost died, and that yesterday she had entered me in a preteen beauty contest. I reminded her that my pubic bone was broken, but she said she had already tracked down a sponsor who assured her I would not have to appear in the swimsuit section with any of the other eleven-year-olds or be required to go up or down the auditorium stairs on my crutches.

"They said they'd even put in a ramp if we want," she said, handing me the telephone before she went off with a nurse to sign more papers. "Isn't that terrific?"

My father was supposed to be living in Coos Bay by the water, and most of the time I was the one in charge of calling him. He wasn't usually at his house very much, but since we were in a hospital, I had the operator ring for as long a time as she could, just in case he picked up.

"How did his voice sound?" Bobbie asked when she got back from her errands.

"Okay," I said. "It sounded all right."

On my last day at the Veteran's, Peggy, the physical therapist, taught me how to use the crutches. My job was to practice limping up and down the hallway on alternating legs while she and Bobbie kept the rhythm going with loud claps. In the pharmacy on the first floor, I chose purple armrests for the crutches, and Bobbie bought me flower stickers to paste on the wood. Then, when it was time to go, Kevin walked us over to our car and gave Bobbie his telephone number.

"There are a few choices on here," he said, ripping her off an extra page from his prescription pad, "so give me a buzz anytime."

On the drive home, Bobbie told me everything she knew about our new neighbor. Her name was Mrs. Linkabaugh; her ex-husband, Bill Linkabaugh, was not allowed within 1,000 feet of her house by order of the Oregon State police; and on the day she finally moved in, Mrs. Linkabaugh handed out at least fifty flyers with Bill Linkabaugh's picture on them just to warn everybody.

"And I want you and your brother to be very careful of characters like these," Bobbie said, cutting off a delivery truck on her way into the carpool lane, "because North Willamette is going downhill."

North Willamette is our street. When we were with my father, we lived on North Amherst, North Lombard, and North McCrum. Now Bobbie says she'll never move again, not even if North Willamette becomes a slum.

Mrs. Linkabaugh's new house used to belong to Oliver Grevitch, who died trying to put up his storm windows. One Saturday he got out his ladder and climbed all the way up the side of his house and had a thrombosis. Bobbie's boyfriend Dale was in the driveway when it happened, and he says Mr. Grevitch hung on to his ladder the whole time and the two of them fell together, just like a chopped-down tree.

"Light me a cigarette, will you?" said Bobbie. "This bitch in the Gold Duster won't get off my ass."

When I got it lit, I tapped her, and she held out her hand so I could stick it between the right fingers. The woman in the Gold Duster leaned on the horn, but Bobbie ignored her and smoked with her tip out the window. When the honking got louder, she stuck her middle finger in the rearview mirror.

"This woman can eat me," she said, punching down the automatic lock button and pulling us back into the exit lane. "Now, roll up your window and hold on, we're taking Killingsworth."

I turned down the radio and kept my eyes on the floor mats, because Killingsworth and Alberta were bad avenues. The summer lifeguard at Peninsula Park used to tell everybody in the free swim that carloads of men from Killingsworth kidnapped girls like us all the time and did it to them over and over in the double-doggy style.

When we got to Lombard Street and into downtown St. John's, Bobbie drove past the Coronet store, where Dale was the assistant manager.

"Honk and wave!" she said, but I left my hands at my sides. The last time we visited Dale at work, he was refusing to give somebody a refund on a stuffed animal. The man asked for store credit, but Dale pulled a pencil out of his red apron and pointed it at the man's chest.

"That's not our policy at Coronet, buddy," he said. "No refunds. No exchanges."

Bobbie leaned across the gear shift, trying to see in through the big double doors. "Wave!" she said. "Why aren't you waving?"

"Because nobody will see me."

"Well, that is a really nice thing," she said, jamming down the gas and pulling us back out into the road, "considering Dale paid for your pubic bone."

"He did not."

"Oh yes he did."

I told her he didn't. My fractures were covered by our family health insurance, or paid for by my grandmother Peek.

"Oh, really?" said Bobbie, turning from the wheel and grabbing for another cigarette. "You better have a word with your father about that."

I didn't know what this meant, but there wasn't time to figure it out, because she was digging through her purse, and something large made of poured concrete seemed to be racing toward the car at a dangerous speed, and I said to watch out, watch out, but it was too late, because by then we were driving onto a parking island.

As the tow truck pulled us into our driveway, I saw Mrs. Linkabaugh for the first time. She was on her front porch in a velour mini-robe, sweeping the Astroturf doormat that used to belong to Oliver Grevitch. I stared at her thigh muscles flexing and her big chest swinging around in a nice sort of rhythm.

"Don't look at her!" Bobbie said. "God."

But everybody stared as Mrs. Linkabaugh bent over and

shook out her mat, because she was a lot bigger than Bobbie. Everywhere.

"Jesus Christ," the tow-truck driver said. "Get a load of that shit."

"Well, she doesn't seem too concerned about Psycho Bill today," Bobbie said, waving and smiling at Mrs. Linkabaugh through the tow-truck window. I waved at Mrs. Linkabaugh, too, and she blew me a kiss, shrugging her apologies as the chained Doberman in her yard lunged toward us over and over.

After he got the car unhooked, the tow-truck driver, whose pocket said *I'm Eddie—May I help you?*, didn't even talk to Bobbie. He walked right by the Bill Linkabaugh poster staplegunned to the telephone pole and straight up onto Mrs. Linkabaugh's parking strip to introduce himself. While they were talking, Mrs. Linkabaugh retied her bathrobe two times, and Eddie kept teasing her Doberman with his elbow, making the dog jump up and down like a seal.

Pretty soon, they went into Mrs. Linkabaugh's house, and I imagined her putting on tea to boil and *I'm Eddie—May I help you?* coming up behind her like my father used to do with Bobbie when he lived with us, and while the kettle was screaming, the kitchen table would be bumping and scooting itself all the way across the floor and into another room. But Mrs. Linkabaugh's windows stayed just as dark as Oliver Grevitch's used to be in the old days, and there was nothing to see except the empty tow truck and the Doberman that kept on whining and throwing itself up against her front door.

Bobbie hung our picture of Bill Linkabaugh on the center of the refrigerator. She told Denny and me to watch for him at all times, and if we saw anybody that looked even a bit like him, we were to dial 911. Denny sat with his cap gun aimed out the window until it was time for dinner, and everybody looked at the Bill Linkabaugh poster while we ate. A refrigerator magnet was between his eyes, which made him seem even more threatening.

"I can't look and I can't look away," Bobbie said, staring at the poster. "He's got Son of Sam written all over him."

Denny dipped the tip of his gun in and out of his milk. "Son of who?"

"Sam," said Bobbie. "Son of Sam. And don't make people repeat themselves."

When we were done eating, Bobbie propped me on the couch with all six of her pillows and opened the windows and doors as wide as they would go. She paid Denny five dollars to go to bed early, and while she was watching him get ready, to make sure he didn't brush his teeth with just water or put his pajamas on over his regular clothes, I listened to the crickets and the swishing of the automatic sprinklers that Mrs. Linkabaugh had inherited from Oliver Grevitch. There were eight sprinkler heads in all, installed in two perfect rows of four on the front and back lawns and set to a special timing system that watered each section of the grass in wide, revolving fountains every night at nine-thirty. The night was so quiet, I could even hear stray drops of sprinkler splatter against the side of Mrs. Linkabaugh's house if I listened close enough, and I concentrated on the bright yellow light seeping out through her curtains, wishing they would open up and let me see if she and Eddie were inside listening to the sprinklers, too.

Even when I didn't have a fractured pubic bone, our living room couch was my favorite place to be. From our living room we had a view of the whole street, and especially of our left-side neighbor, because Bobbie had the couch placed right in the nook between two big picture windows at the front corner of our house. And since every house on North Willamette and North Amherst between McCrum and North Woolsey had the exact same floor plan, all the windows of our houses matched up perfectly, with only about eight feet in between. When Oliver Grevitch was alive, he had kept his curtains closed twenty-four hours a day, not like the Bongaards on the other side of us, who never close theirs, ever. The Bongaards were the reason Bobbie had Dale put our satellite dish up in front of her bedroom window, because she said she wanted to be able to let in some light once in a while and not have disgusting Karl Bongaard leering in at her constantly with his moon face.

By the time Denny was tucked in, my pelvis hurt so bad it felt like it might crack in half all over again, so Bobbie gave me an extra pain pill like Kevin told her to, and sat with me for a while on the couch. She held my hand, and we looked through some of her beauty-contest picture albums together. Most of them were of her winning, and not expecting to, and screaming, and having her eye makeup streak down, but tonight there was one I'd never seen before stuck in with all the rest. Instead of being up on a stage with a bunch of other girls, in this one she was totally alone, standing on a stepladder under an orange tree and reaching up to pick one. There wasn't any makeup on her face, and her bangs fell straight down into her eyes without curls. She had on a dirty white tank top with cutoff jeans, and the mosquito bites on her legs were scabbed over from too much scratching.

"What's that one?" I asked.

"Just me on a picnic," she said, turning the page, but I turned it back.

"With who? You look messy and nice."

"I don't even know with who," she said, smoothing down the plastic page where it was bubbling a little around the edges. "Let's check what's on TV."

After Mrs. Linkabaugh let in her Doberman, Bobbie went next door to get the bill from *I'm Eddie—May I help you?*, but nobody answered her knock. She came back after a while, and I lit her three cigarettes before she threw up her hands.

"What should I do?" she asked. "Call a tow truck to tow a fucking tow truck?"

Then Denny came back out wearing only his pajama bottoms, so Bobbie got her five dollars back and said we could both watch *Rat Patrol* reruns until midnight. She didn't go out with Dale, either, and we got to eat as many bowls of Honeycomb as we wanted, until my stomach pressed way out like a fist. Halfway through the second episode, Bobbie went into the kitchen and had a phone fight with Dale because he wouldn't come over. She told him to kiss her ass and then sat on the receiver.

"Go ahead, you prick! Come on," she said.

But when she put her ear back to the phone, we could tell from the look on her face that he'd already hung up.

Most of the time Dale doesn't spend the night over here because he has to be at the Coronet putting prices on things by nine A.M. He says he likes it better when Bobbie spends the night at his apartment over on Germantown Road so he can know exactly where all his stuff is and use his own shower and towels. Denny and I have never been over to Germantown Road, but Bobbie says the only thing Dale's got over there that we don't is a WaterPik, and that his shower is probably where she got ringworm.

I was allowed to stay on the couch for the whole night and take one more half of a pain pill just in case. After I'd swallowed it with orange juice, Bobbie emptied the whole bottle onto the coffee table, chopped the rest of the pills in half with a butter knife, and locked all of them in the same drawer of her dresser where she keeps the pills Denny takes for his attention span.

Our old babysitter Crystal was the one who figured out he was hyperactive. One night when Bobbie was gone, she was talking to her daughter Crissy long-distance in California, and while she wasn't looking, Denny climbed up on the couch and started jumping so high he flew up and cracked his head open on the ceiling. Crystal hung right up on Crissy, and we screamed and screamed at him to stop, but Denny kept bouncing up and down, up and down, with the blood running into his ears until we pinned him to the carpet. Then, when Bobbie got to the emergency room, Crystal explained to her that Denny was at least as hyper as her son Ray used to be, and that we had better give him Ritalin. I know for a fact my father was the one who paid for all of that.

It was late by the time Eddie left Mrs. Linkabaugh's. By then everybody was asleep but me, because I like to watch the raccoons come up from Mock's Crest Marsh and go through the garbage cans in the back alley. Sometimes whole families come. I've seen them eat cake mix and raw eggs and Tender Vittles cat food. Usually, I get to put out a bowl of water for them, too, because we heard they like to wash their food. But tonight the alley was empty except for Eddie, who spit on Mrs. Linkabaugh's grass before he got inside his truck and peeled out, on his way to another accident.

On regular nights, I wake up two or three times, but because of Kevin's pill, I slept the whole night on the couch without waking up once. When I opened my eyes, Bobbie was sitting in the La-Z-Boy with Denny on her lap. She was smoking and staring out the window with the tow-truck bill still in her hand.

"There's living proof that the *Penthouse* letters are true," she said, pointing the burning end of her cigarette at Mrs. Linkabaugh's driveway. "Bad timing for *you-know-who.*"

"You-know-who doesn't want to live with us," said Denny, swinging his legs back and forth and making the chair bounce. "You-know-who wants to live in Coos Bay."

Bobbie reached up in the air and grabbed one of his ankles. "What did I tell you, Denny," she asked, "about sitting still?"

"You told me to try it."

"That's exactly right," said Bobbie, dropping his leg and looking back out the window. "So practice what I preach."

When my father moved to Coos Bay, Bobbie put all his *Penthouse*s in a Hefty bag down in the basement next to the pup tent Denny and I got from saving Green Stamps. She said he only read them to torture her because of her small chest. Besides the *Penthouse*s, my father also read *Hustler*, *Roadie*, and *Big on Top*, so I'm sure Bobbie was right about him liking Mrs. Linkabaugh.

After breakfast Bobbie gave me her July *Cosmopolitan* to read for the rest of the morning, and in the afternoon she taught me how to do the wave. She said the wave is the most important part of the beauty contest, twice as important as what a person says.

"The judges absolutely loved my wave," she said, cupping her hand and fluttering the fingers up and down in her famous way. "So you've got to do it, because everybody always waves flat-handed now."

I'd seen Bobbie doing her wave in pictures and to my father a hundred times because when he first saw Bobbie, she was riding a giant float shaped like a Sunkist navel orange in a parade through Rosemont, California. She had waved and waved at him and the big group of people he was standing with, not even knowing that he was going to follow her orange through the crowd, all the way back to the football field where the parade started, and that right after graduation, she was going to wind up in Oregon with him and me and Denny.

Because of how slow I was on the crutches, it took us a long time to get my wave right. We decided to add a wrist swing to my wave that made it more complicated than Bobbie's, and after an hour of waving at each other into the bathroom mirror, switching rooms, and alternating arms, Bobbie decided I ought to try it out on Mrs. Linkabaugh, who was outside in purple short shorts, hosing down her camper.

"Pick a point above her head to focus on," Bobbie said, standing beside me at the window and holding on to my extra crutch. "Then go through the whole thing one step at a time."

We tried all kinds of combinations to get her attention, but Mrs. Linkabaugh was too busy cleaning the inside of the wheel wells to notice.

"Those waves are looking totally perfect," Bobbie said, staring out at Mrs. Linkabaugh, who was bending down to spray underneath the cab. "She's just not the type to appreciate them."

After Mrs. Linkabaugh went inside, I thought Bobbie and I would keep working on my waves until dinner, but Denny came home from day camp, and Dale called to convince Bobbie to go out, so she took the phone into her bedroom. I figured they were talking about my pelvis money, too, because the phone cord was pulled as tight as it would go and I couldn't hear anything they were saying through the door.

Denny took off his socks and shoes and sat down next to me on the couch to wait for Bobbie, and we watched Mrs. Linkabaugh's camper drip-drying in the sun together. It was covered with hunting stickers, and a pair of mossy-green antlers were bolted to the top of the cab that made it look weird and alive. It was easy to imagine Bill Linkabaugh dragging the dead owner of those antlers through the dark woods, home to wherever he and Mrs. Linkabaugh had lived.

"Check out the gun rack," Denny said, pointing at the window right behind the driver's seat. "It was his truck for sure."

He took off the house key on a string that Bobbie made him wear to day camp, and swung it around like a lasso. "Bill Linkabaugh is coming back to get it with a gun."

I stared at Denny and the horned half-animal camper, suddenly remembering the possible danger we could all be in, picturing Bobbie and Dale out playing pool while Bill Linkabaugh ripped down our screen door with the butt end of a hunting rifle.

"You better go get Bobbie off the phone," I said, keeping my eyes glued to the camper. "Now."

Denny threw down his house key and hit the floor at a dead run.

"*Bobbbbie!*" he called, slapping her bedroom door over and over again with a flat hand. "Bill Linkabaugh is coming over here tonight with a gun."

Bobbie's door cracked open slowly, just enough to let out her head. She covered the receiver and bent down to Denny's level, putting a hand on his shoulder and talking to him very slowly, right into the face like he was deaf, too, and not just hyperactive. "Denny," she said, nodding while she talked and looking him straight in the eye, "it only says that on a poster."

"Well, it's a police poster, Bobbie," said Denny, crossing his arms. "You better tell Dale that poster was made by the Oregon State Police."

Bobbie stood up and looked at the ceiling. She took a deep breath and let it out in a long sigh. "Dale is very aware of that, Denny, thank you," she said, pulling her head back into the bedroom. "Thank you very much."

Denny came over to the couch and shoved the crutches into my hands. "It's a police poster," he said.

I stood in front of Bobbie's door for a long time and stared down at my feet. They were barely even touching the carpet at all, dangling like lead weights between the two fat rubber traction cups on the bottom of my crutches. Kevin had told us I was supposed to feel normal after the second day, but as my fist knocked on Bobbie's door, the whole top half of my body seemed way too loose and light all of a sudden, like everything on me from the waist up was rising, shooting up into the air with a rush, like a helium balloon.

"Bobbie," I said, in my calmest voice. "Open the door."

I heard the receiver click, and Bobbie was standing over me immediately. She was smiling, but everything on her face said that if Bill Linkabaugh or the blurry ache in my pelvis didn't kill me, then she definitely would.

"What?" she asked.

Karl Bongaard's lawn mower started up outside, and I closed my eyes, listening to the horrible chopping sound it made, preparing for death.

"Bobbie!" I yelled over all the noise. "Bobbie?"

Bobbie looked over at Denny for a minute and then back at me as if we were crazy. "What?" she screamed back. *"What?"*

Through the window behind her, I could see parts of Karl Bongaard's body jerking by as he followed his lawn mower from one end of his grass to the other.

"Well," I said, focusing hard on her kneecaps. "My wave is not ready for the contest. And Denny and I think you ought to stay home tonight."

Bobbie leaned back against the doorjamb and crossed her arms, listening to the lawn mower roar practically up to the edge of our house, then move away.

"Really?" she asked, looking me up and down and straight in the eye. "That's what the two of you think, huh?"

"Yep," said Denny, before I could stop him. "That's what we think. Her wave sucks, and Bill Linkabaugh is on the loose, and you better stay home and get us dinner."

"Well, Denny," said Bobbie, walking past me into the kitchen, "you can tell your sister I'm not staying home tonight. For her information, this kind of behavior is called pressure, and I get enough of that from Dale."

"Then what are we supposed to eat?" I yelled after her. "If you're always going out and leaving us here?"

A cupboard door slammed, and another one opened.

"Tell your sister she's having Potato Buds and a green vegetable, Denny," she called from inside the refrigerator. "And that she had better stop rattling my cage."

Dale honked when the Potato Buds were still lumpy, and by that time, we had made Bobbie feel bad. She turned up the burners, dumped in the rest of the milk, and gave Denny a bigger spatula to stir with.

"Whip them, precious. Whip them!" she said, digging through her purse for the number of the pay phone at the Billiard Club. She leaned out the screen door and held up three fingers to Dale, which meant to wait three minutes before honking again.

"What you can do is call information for the number after I go," she said. "You know what to ask for—it's in St. John's."

She handed me each of our pill halves and twelve dollars for a cab fare in case of an emergency, but I didn't even look at her.

"Doors and windows are to be locked by ten," she said, reaching back to zip up the rest of her dress. "But I'll probably be home long before then. Okay?"

I stared out the window and whispered that I didn't care. I might be calling Coos Bay.

"Excuse me, madame," Bobbie said, cupping her hand around her ear like she was hard of hearing. "Is that a threat?"

But I only shook my head and concentrated on the dirt patch in the front yard where my swing set used to be.

Dale leaned on the horn.

"Don't test me, either of you," Bobbie said. "Because Coos Bay is a fucking joke."

Denny stirred the potatoes without looking up, and I peeled a flower sticker off one of my crutches.

"Well, this is just great, isn't it?" Bobbie said, slamming a new stick of butter down in the center of the table. "I guess the sooner I go, the sooner he can bring me home."

"Yep," said Denny, continuing to stir. "And then Bill Linkabaugh can come over and kill us."

Bobbie marched over and grabbed her open purse off the coffee table. "I can promise you Bill Linkabaugh isn't going to be killing anybody, Denny," she said, checking the contents before she snapped it shut. "The swamp thing next door only wishes he was that desperate."

Denny brought dinner over to the couch, and we ate without mentioning Bill Linkabaugh or even looking at his poster. After dinner he got us water for our pills, rinsed the dishes, and made sure all the burners were off. I had him put some leftover Potato Buds out for the raccoons and was about ready to have him lock up early and turn on all our stand-up fans when we heard Otis Redding coming from next door. It was one of Bobbie's favorite songs, "(Sittin' On) The Dock of the Bay," and it floated in through Mrs. Linkabaugh's wide-open bedroom curtains, where she was sitting on the edge of her furry red water bed with a man.

Both of us could see that she was listening very carefully to him, nodding at whatever he said, understanding him perfectly. In fact, the strength of all her yesses was even rocking the water bed a little, making it seem like the two of them were riding in a boat.

Denny ran to lock the doors and brought the Bill Linkabaugh poster in from the refrigerator, but from the back of the head, we couldn't tell a thing about the man on the bed at all except that he slicked back his hair.

I slid down on the couch as far as I could go, and Denny crouched next to me with his chin on the sill. "Screw Coos Bay," he whispered, "we're calling the cops as soon as he turns around."

I nodded. "As soon as he turns around."

I stared down at the poster until my eyes started to swim, trying to memorize everything about Bill Linkabaugh's face and ignore the red words printed beside his left cheek: *MAY BE ARMED.* There was a buzz inside my ear, as if someone had turned on a tiny blow dryer. And I remembered Kevin's pill that was probably going to make me fall asleep long before the police could even get their squad cars to our house.

Denny closed one eye and aimed at the man's head with an imaginary gun. "If that's Bill," he said, "he's gonna be sorry he was ever born."

I covered Denny's mouth with my hand. "Stop talking," I said, "or I'll kill you."

Mrs. Linkabaugh was wearing the same short shorts she'd had on earlier, but with a new halter top made out of yellow bandannas. Right near the end of the song, when Otis was sighing and breathing and humming, she grabbed the man's head, pushing it against her chest, and the two of them stood up and started dancing, swaying back and forth on each other like they'd had too much to drink.

"How tall does it say he is?" Denny asked, grabbing the poster out of my hands. "I think he's too short to be Bill."

"Bill is five-eleven, one-eighty," I said, grabbing the poster back and giving Denny a charley horse. "We have to look at him from the front."

The man flipped Mrs. Linkabaugh around and started dancing with her from behind. He reached around and put a hand across her eyebrows and pulled her head back to rest on his shoulder, burying his whole face in her hair.

Her neck was bent back at a bad angle, like maybe he was about to break it, but then, right after "Midnight Train to Georgia" started, Mrs. Linkabaugh said something to the man that made him let go, and they both started to laugh out loud, quietly at first, then deep from the belly, like what was happening in that room had to be the most hysterical thing in the whole wide world.

"We better do something," Denny said, but neither of us moved. All we could manage was to watch without breathing, pressing our faces closer and closer to the window screen until I was sure we were both going to smother.

It took them forever to get over laughing, but when they finally did, Mrs. Linkabaugh grabbed the man by the arm and dragged him out onto the back patio. She hooked her screen door to the side of the house, and a giant pool of buttery light spilled onto the lawn. Then she jumped down the steps and backed farther and farther out onto Oliver Grevitch's thick summer grass, gesturing for the man to follow, holding out both hands. But he didn't move an inch.

"Charlotte," he called to her from the top of the porch steps. "Charlotte, c'mere."

But Mrs. Linkabaugh ignored him and kept on going.

"Her name's Charlotte," Denny whispered, and we both ducked our heads below the windowsill for a minute and said her name out loud. "Charlotte Linkabaugh."

And in the fuzzy shadow glow that surrounded her, from the streetlight and the porch light and the light of the moon, Mrs. Charlotte Linkabaugh reached down and slipped off her sling-back sandals, tossing them over her shoulders out into the dark, one at a time.

Once the man saw that, he came down the porch steps right away, but before he could get even halfway across the yard, she ran up in her bare feet and jumped on him, wrapping her legs around his waist and letting him dance her around and around in circles. The man arched his body backward to hold up all the weight, turning her faster and faster and faster like an ice skater, until everybody lost track of the time except for Oliver Grevitch's automatic sprinklers, which blasted out of the ground right on schedule.

Then, in the middle of the water that seemed to be spewing everywhere, in the middle of Mrs. Linkabaugh's terrible half-hyena scream, the surprised man froze just for a second, and he looked up at the sky as if he was very confused about where all the water was coming from, and as he stood there in front of us, with his eyes searching the air above his head, there was no disputing anymore who he was.

"Holy Christ," said Denny. "Bill."

I nodded. "Bill," I said. "It's Bill."

And while we stared out at the yard next door, trying to make our calculations about which police to call, and how many, and when, the Linkabaughs were running through their own sprinklers, illegally.

They had both started laughing again but sillier, dizzier, this time, uncontrolled. Both of them soaked through all their clothes, chasing each other around like they'd never figured out how good cold water could feel in the middle of July.

One time on the way around the yard, when Bill was chasing her with his belt, swinging it around his head and snapping it behind her like a wet towel, I saw Mrs. Linkabaugh jump through a burst of water like a track hurdler. Her hair was plastered to her cheeks and her arm was stretched way up above her head, reaching high like Bobbie in the messy white tank top, trying to grab for that orange on the ladder back in California, and as I waited for her to come back down, to land again on the slippery grass, I wished the hot night could stretch out forever, because I knew that, like Bobbie, she would probably never be up in the air like that again.

Get Away from
Me, David

There was an earthquake at the bank this morning: totally minor, maybe a 3. This is peanuts for the central valley, but the tellers, I swear to you, acted like it was the fall of Pompeii. When the first jolt knocked some ten key machines to the floor, Windows 4 and 5 completely lost their shit, clutching onto their countertops, screaming. After that, the hysteria really caught on, and it wasn't very long before all eight of them were bunched up in a little herd back against the safe.

I'd like to say for the record right now: This was nothing close to a natural disaster. It was like sitting down on a cheap vibrator bed for about fifteen seconds, if you want to know the truth.

What really happened was there was this incredibly loud clang when some of the stanchions in the merchant line fell over. They do this plenty of times without seismic help. The only problem was that there happened to be an elderly customer hanging on to those stanchions when they went down. This caused José Martinson, the lending manager, to come striding out of his office like a superhero, and like a superhero, José Martinson had to sweep this customer up off the linoleum and usher this gentleman, a perfectly fine-seeming person of the Mexican persuasion in an Izod sweatsuit, to one of the folding chairs along the wall next to the drinking fountain.

I should mention, by the way, that when I saw the guy in the sweatsuit fall down, I was planning to go provide whatever assistance I could in this nonemergency, but José stopped me as he whisked past my desk. "No, David," he said. "You sit down. You hang on to your monitor right now."

Actually, the way José delivered that sentence, it sounded more like "Youhangontoyourmonitorrightnow."

In a perfect world, i.e., one in which I didn't work at the Bouquet Canyon Bank of Modesto for José Martinson, I would turn to this man I didn't work for, and when he said something like "You hang on to your monitor right now," I would say something like "YOUSUCKMYCOCKRIGHTNOW."

But the world was and is not perfect, so at that point I looked at José and smiled and cast a silent and negative spell on his family for all of eternity. "Sure, José," I said, and as he walked away from the lending area, I wondered if this was going to be the day in which I took just one tiny sip of the Vicks DayQuil that I've been storing behind the mortgage refinancing forms in the second drawer of my desk.

By then the plate glass on the front and sides of the bank was quivering quite a bit, too, and it was kind of exciting to wonder whether or not the whole place was going to shatter like a wineglass. I'm a person who does well with a lot of physical stimulation, so I found the whole thing to be pretty invigorating myself.

I opened up the top drawer of my desk, and instead of the DayQuil, I ate four baby aspirin from the slide-open package with the tin soldiers on it that I keep up front by the writing utensils for class-B situations. I knew the baby aspirins were not going to alter my physiognomy in the least, but I took them anyway, even though I could barely swallow them due to the situation of the earth moving around like it was. I also figured the placebo would give me courage to do what I had really set out to do before the absolutely harmless earthquake started, which was to, actually, in reality, walk across the linoleum floor toward the front entrance of the bank and approach the official work area of the not exactly beautiful but still strangely compelling security guard, Elizabeth Sabretta, in the cowboy boots and the badly bitten-down hangnails, who, ever since her divorce settlement finally came through, drives a silver Honda Accord with a little bumper sticker in the shape of a yield sign pasted to the rear window that says: GODDESS ON BOARD.

At the thought of that bumper sticker, I popped an extra aspirin, and then I put my arms around my computer like José told me to, and as I hugged it tightly against my chest, I wondered, if I was *not* able to walk across the floor of the bank today toward Elizabeth Sabretta due to the earthquake, was it going to be the day in which, actually, in reality, I was to take just one tiny sip from the aforementioned Vicks DayQuil, just to see what might happen. Just to see if maybe I'd end up back in Strawberry, New Mexico, where I used to be completely involved in My Old Life, which was drunken and miserable rather than just sober and miserable like it is now.

I considered taking out the DayQuil right then, just to look at it maybe, to consider the possibility of complete and utter self-ruination just for a sec, but right then I couldn't do that, because during the whole time José was helping the old man brush off, during the whole time he was getting the old man out of the way and seating him in the chair for safety, José kept glancing over at me with this look on his face that said: "David—you should be me right now," and I had no choice but to glance back in a dishonest way that said: "José, you're probably right," even though we both know José has no idea how to delegate. He's what my sponsor, Nate, would call "an angry and resentful doer."

As I said, the shaking didn't go on for that long, but after it stopped, everybody was still frozen in their places like right before a shootout. José has the place decorated like an old ghost town, with wagon wheels and other western-style items, and I could swear at that moment I saw some tumbleweed blowing across the floor and butting up against the ankles of the old man, who was sitting right in the chair where José had propped him, like a knickknack.

"Stay still for aftershocks," José called out to everybody.

The tellers started to whimper when he said it, but the whole thing was fine by me. I kept my arms around my computer monitor, and I faced directly toward the front entrance, where Elizabeth Sabretta was standing with her spine straight as a parking meter, her feet planted shoulder width apart, her knees bent slightly, and her arms braced on either side of the doorjamb, i.e., exactly like it says to do in the "Earthquakes in the Workplace" brochure.

Along with her security guard's job, Elizabeth Sabretta is also a cocktail waitress at the Desdemona Room on Buena Viela Avenue in downtown Modesto, and one day I am planning on asking her whether or not she'd mind if I came down there in the evening after ten and had an ice water–no whiskey at some point in the future. She wouldn't have to say when. I've talked about this idea with my sponsor, Nate, who says that given my relationship to bars, this is not such a good idea. I'm not really in the position to argue with Nate to his face, but I am aware that the Desdemona Room is a public establishment. I could go in there in a goddamn bunny suit if I felt like it. As long as I didn't seek chemical enhancement of any kind while I was in there, I could do whatever the fuck I want.

After José got the old man situated, he walked out to the center of the floor and, with a ceremonial flash of his samurai sword, set the stanchions of the merchant line back in place. "Okay, ladies," he said to the tellers, bowing in their direction. "The party's over. Let's get back to work."

There was a round of applause and hysterical laughter from over near the safe, as if what José had said was actually a witticism of some kind. Then he and Windows 1–6 gathered into a huddle and gave one another a group hug while Windows 7 and 8 stood around them clapping. Fortunately, I was not a part of that, but because of my central desk placement, I had to watch the whole thing. José in the middle with all the women cooing around him, touching his sweater with their fingertips, fixing his hair.

When José was done with the teller treatment, he went over to Elizabeth Sabretta, who was still frozen in the doorjamb. He put a hand on her shoulder, shook it a little, and said, "Hey. Everything okay out here?" and Elizabeth Sabretta nodded at him slightly and said, "I guess so. Yeah."

I didn't realize I was still holding on to the computer until José swept past my desk and gave me a slap on the back. "Thanks for your help back there, David," he said. "You can let go now if you want to. It's over, guy."

"Don't ever touch me," I wanted to say to José. "Don't ever call me *guy*." But I can't get into it with José, because he is actually two people. One is José, and the other is his corporate enthusiasm, which is so large and lifelike it's like a twin brother walking alongside of him. When José talks about the bank in staff meetings sometimes, the glowing terms he uses bring tears of embarrassment to my eyes. I cannot decide if this utter lack of skepticism is real or the result of medication, but I find it disconcerting. Whenever I bring José the paperwork for anything, a loan for a new sunroom on a home or a new billiard table, he falls all over himself thanking me.

"This isn't sales, José," I want to tell him. "This is the economy."

Modesto is growing like a weed bed these days, and we're giving money out to practically anybody who asks. It's a town of white-collar Robin Hoods with bandannas across their faces, I swear to God. In my suit and tie, I sit across from people who have no prospect of ever paying me back for what I'm giving them and no idea what is going on behind my face. They have no idea how easy it would be for me to open that DayQuil, take it down in one swallow, and run out into the endless desert sunshine with all their money gobbed in my fists. I wish someone would punish me for my sins. I don't know what's wrong with this country.

I watched José hustle past me into his glass office, which is located about seven feet from the back of my skull. It's soundproof in José's office, and even though I couldn't hear him, I could still feel him darting around back there, getting things done. I let go of my computer and sort of hunched over my blotter, trying not to let José's activity get to me.

In the doorway, Elizabeth Sabretta took out her blood-pressure kit. She set the works on the stool José has given her for that purpose and took out the armband attached to the curly black tube. I watched her roll up the sleeve of her security uniform and cinch the armband tight around her upper arm. Elizabeth Sabretta has arrhythmia, so she is supposed to check her blood pressure several times a day and sometimes more if she is under particular stress. This is entirely amazing to watch, especially the part where she flexes the arm up and down and the air squeezes out of the little black bag.

I was imagining this might be a good time to walk over there and say something to her like "Hey. Everything okay out here?" and she could nod slightly and say something like "I guess so. Yeah," but just then José materialized again.

"David," he said. "Do you know what day it is?"

I shook my head.

"Oh, come on." José came around to my side of the desk. He did it so fast I didn't have time to react. "Stand up, David," he said. "I want to shake your hand."

Even sitting down, I was a head taller than José. I am a large man, but I am not at all powerful. José put a hand on each of my shoulders and kind of pulled me out of my chair. It was a strange motion, because it felt like my chair was sucking me down at the same rate that José was yanking me up. That chair is like one of those NASA anti-gravity things. Sometimes I can work a whole morning without getting up once.

José put his arms around my waist. "I want to welcome you, David," he said. "Your probation period. It's over, man. How does it feel to be a full-time hire?"

I looked down at the top of his head. José took a step back. His eyes were bright. He reached out and took one of my hands and clasped it in both of his. My fingers were sticky from the baby aspirin. "Tell me, David," he said, and then he was back in my arms, so close to me his words were muffled against my shirt front. "How does it feel?"

Tucked beneath my chin, the top of José's head was perfectly round. I imagined reaching inside his skull and pulling out his brain. I imagined taking a bite out of it like an apple and then being poisoned by all the chemical well-being that must reside in there and then being buried in a pine coffin out by the airfield and having strangers walking by the grave marker where I was and saying, "Look at that loan-officer guy who ate a branch manager's brain and died."

"It feels good," I said.

José beamed. "Those are the words I wanted to hear, because today I'm leaving you in charge of the girls during the lunch period."

I should mention that when José said the words, "in charge," I felt the little blip in my head that my sponsor, Nate, says to watch out for. The blip is chemical and feels like a small electric shock, or a pinch maybe, of all the neurons in my frontal lobe. When I feel the blip in my brain, I have to do something right away. Like go outside into the parking lot behind the Dumpster and do some jumping jacks or go put my head under the faucet in the bathroom.

I blinked slowly and took some time to get back to José regarding his needs. "In charge?" I said.

José took a hold of my shoulders and squeezed them. "Don't worry, buddy," he said. "I'm only going over to Cattlemen's, across the street. I'll take the booth by the window. If you need me, you can just run across and get me, okay?"

I thought of the DayQuil in the second drawer. I could smell José's cologne all over me. I thought of what it would be like to go over one night in a ninja costume to José's cul-de-sac, abduct his golden retrievers, and drag them away in a gunnysack.

"I'll keep that in mind," I said to him. "Have a nice lunch."

Because I was a new employee and could not be left alone on the premises, José and I usually took joint lunches in the conference room together. This was supposed to go on indefinitely until I was trained. I agreed with José, of course, about my Inability to Run a Bank, even though, as you can imagine, these lunches were no fun. Most of the time José talked about his children, who are well-adjusted little people, and his wife, who loves him. My goal was to sit as quietly as I could until the lunchtime was over and imagine myself saying things to José like "What if you woke up next to your wife tomorrow and she was dead?" or "Do your kids have all the right numbers of fingers and toes?"

Now I wanted those old days back, when I just sat and chewed my pot stickers across from José and wiped my fingers on the underside of the table when he wasn't looking. I did not want to be left in charge. I was left in charge of a family back in Strawberry, New Mexico, and look what happened there.

I adjusted the blotter on my desk. "You go to lunch," I heard myself saying. "You have fun."

José smiled. "Well, I'm only going across the street—it's not going to be that fun, is it?"

I attempted to shrug at José, but it felt more like a wince. The patchy soy field outside my window was suddenly starting to expand, stetching around the building like a green sea. It was also hard to locate the horizon line at the moment because the earth happened to be the same murk-brown as the sky. It was something you had to estimate. My body was throbbing like an infected gum. "It'll be fine," I said.

José patted me on the shoulder. He went back into his office and shut the door. I swiveled around in my chair and watched him go. I watched him picking up his coat and keys. It was only a matter of time before he stranded me in a half-irrigated desert with nine women and an unopened bottle. The backs of my pant legs were plastered against the seat of my chair. Things inside the bank had an echoey feel. People's shoes clicking on the floor sounded like gunshots. Regular talking sounded like little screams.

I glanced out at the soy field again. Just quickly. But this is when I saw her. The Woman I Used to Love, standing in the rows, in the sleeveless nylon dress. She was up to her knees in green plants. Just standing there. But we saw each other. I know we did.

I turned my back on the window, but I could feel her ghost eyes behind me, staring. I reached for the telephone on my desk. It felt like I was tackling it. It was like a rabbit about to leap out of my hands. The floor of the bank was starting to change shape as I moved. Things were swelling up and then shrinking down.

I knew the number by heart, even though I'd never dialed it before. Not from work. The phone rang seven times. I could hear a burst of canned laughter from the TV in the background when he answered.

"Hey, Nate," I said.

"Oh, hey, David," Nate said, without an inkling of surprise. "What's going on?"

For about five months now, Nate has been asking me to call him whenever things get iffy, but I never do. Mostly because I think Nate has family money, and I know he'll be there watching his 500 channels of cable, and I can't stand the image of him sitting there in his shower thongs, not having to work.

"Talk to me, David," Nate said. "What's up?"

I pressed my hand against the outside of the second drawer and watched the fingers turn white. "Oh, nothing," I said. "I'm just here at the bank."

"That doesn't sound very convincing," Nate said. "Why are you whispering?"

I cupped my hand around the receiver and bent over it. "Because I just saw her," I said.

There was a silence on the line. "Who?"

"You know."

Nate paused. "David," he asked. "Are you alone over there?"

"She's standing behind me right now," I said. "Outside the window."

I could hear whatever chair Nate was sitting in creak loudly as he sat up. "Listen, David," he said. "I'm right here. Repeat it after me. 'I'm not alone.'"

"I'm not alone," I said.

"There," Nate said. "How does that feel?"

The phone receiver in my hand was hard and white. It felt like I was holding a human femur up to my ear and talking into it. Then I saw José, looming toward my desk.

He had his driving gloves on and his briefcase and his reflector sunglasses. He looked like a cross between Ozzie Nelson and Freddie Prinze. He was moving fast, too, and a small whirlwind was forming in his wake.

"I have to go, Nate," I said.

"See you, buddy," José said as he swashbuckled on by. "Don't forget to come across the street if you need me. Literally, just come out into the parking lot and wave. I'll see you. I won't take my eyes off the bank."

I opened my mouth to say something, but no words came out.

"Be good girls," José called to the tellers. "David's in charge."

When he said that, the tellers all looked at me blankly. Elizabeth Sabretta did not turn around. "Bye, boss," she said.

I watched José start up his car and drive it over to Cattlemen's across the intersection. Then I took out some Flintstones vitamins from the file cabinet. My hands were shaking pretty badly, but I was able to count out three Bettys and four Wilmas and eat them. Then I poured all of them out and separated the Freds and Barneys and set them in a pile by my phone.

On their way out to smoke, Windows 4 and 5, two of the most popular tellers we have here, brushed past my desk in the lending area and asked Elizabeth Sabretta if she wanted to go with them, but Elizabeth Sabretta only laughed.

"You know me, girl," Elizabeth Sabretta said to Window 4, without even looking up from her magazine. "I don't fraternize with you bitches."

There was a burst of admiring laughter from the tellers, and I could feel my eyes well up with tears of wonder. Elizabeth Sabretta's presence in the world makes me cry without trying. She is all that is left of the American West.

I pressed my fingers into my temples and sat perfectly still in hopes that nothing would make me move. With José gone, the bank felt hysterical. It was like we were on an old stagecoach that was running away downhill without any horses. Suddenly, the whole place was filled with strange women and people. Elizabeth held the door open for everybody. She had a nice word for every single one of them.

Some of the customers I've given money to waved when

they came in. One guy, I swear, looked like he was wearing a pumpkin head. His mouth was gaping open when he smiled.

I took out my little sign that says *I'm sorry, I'm not in right now,* and put it in the center of my blotter, where it was visible to anybody who wanted anything from me. Then I got up from my desk and started to slowly evacuate the area. I did it quietly, imperceptibly, like a dust mote. I just crossed my arms behind my back and began to drift away. I didn't know where I was going, exactly, but I was intercepted from the back by Window 7, the merchant teller. She popped out of the break room and caught me unawares.

"Excuse me," Window 7 said. I turned, and she was standing there with her arms outstretched. "Hi."

She had a stack of white papers in her arms that I didn't recognize. I looked up at her as coolly as I could. Yet I did not reach for what she was holding out. I didn't want to touch anything if I didn't know what it was.

"What are those?" I said.

Window 7 seemed taken aback. She held out the papers even more forcefully.

I felt the floor sink down a couple of inches. I thought I could briefly remember what to do with the paper that Window 7 was handing me, but I did not want to be handed anything. I felt like I had already been handed enough.

"Wait here just a minute," I said to Window 7. "Don't move."

I returned to my desk. I opened the drawer where the DayQuil lay like a sleeping valentine. When I picked it up, I heard the liquid gloop against the sides of the plastic bottle. I put it in the pocket of my suit jacket, then looked over at Window 7, who was still standing where I'd left her, a bottle blonde with teddy-bear barrettes who has millions of dollars passing through her hands each day and has never, as far as I know, made even one significant error.

I angled my body away from Window 7 and began to walk. Fast. I didn't know where I was going at first, but once I saw

José's glass office waiting empty, I went straight for it. The DayQuil banged against my leg. I had to put a hand on it to hold it there.

As soon as she saw me take off, Window 7 was on my tail. It was all I could do not to break into a run. I was about to reach for José's doorknob when she overtook me. We were standing face-to-face like in a western showdown. I imagined slamming the door on her. I pictured her on the outside of that door, banging on it, trying to be let in.

"José buzzed me before he left," Window 7 said breathlessly. "He said you're the one in charge. He said give them to you."

I imagined curling up in a ball in the center of José's brown carpet and facing the rear partition until he came back. But instead, out of nowhere, another guy I know who lives inside me lately and takes care of important business, such as functioning in the rational world, this completely rational guy, he remembered that what he was being handed were the noon receipts. An item the guy was handed practically every day.

"Sorry," this guy said to Window 7. "I'll take those. I don't know what I was thinking."

Then, once the noon receipts were in my hand, the rational guy, he just kind of sauntered out of the bank and left me standing there, like he was off to honeymoon in Strawberry, New Mexico, or something.

I walked to the absolute center of José's office holding the noon receipts. I knew I was allowed in there, but still, I felt like a trespasser. I watched business taking place on the other side of the glass, and it seemed hostile out there. Like a war zone. People were punching on the ATM machines as if the buttons were little detonators. Three or four of these individuals even approached my desk, saw the *I'm not in right now* sign, and then sat down in my mini–living room to wait. Pretty soon they started to talk amongst themselves. I shut José's door and locked it. I was going to sweat them out.

The benefits of José's office were several. He had a much better chair. He also had seven video cameras that zoomed in on every angle of the bank. If I moved over behind José's desk, for instance, I could watch Elizabeth Sabretta in an extreme close-up, sitting on the stool José gave her, eating a Carl's Jr. from a brown bag. It was meditative, watching her eat and wipe her fingers on the napkin. I started chewing in rhythm along with her. Pretending to swallow when she did.

I would give anything to be digested by Elizabeth Sabretta. Anything.

That's what I was doing when there was another knock on the door. When I looked up, Window 7 was gone, and Window 4, the Teller Queen with the confetti fingernails, was standing there instead.

Apparently, this was the kind of lunch hour where trouble was going to metastasize.

I unlocked the door and cracked it open. Window 4 took a step forward.

"Um, David," she said. "Your name is David, right?"

I thought of telling her no, just to see what she'd do, but decided against it. I stayed in the doorway.

Window 4 averted her eyes. "Okay, well, David. We just think that guy, he shouldn't be able to sleep here all day, you know?"

I kept my eyes away from the soy field. "What guy?" I said.

Window 4 raised her head to look at me as if I might have arrived from another planet. "You know," she said, pointing in the direction of the drinking fountain. "The guy who fell."

I stepped around her out of José's office. The man in the tennis visor was still sleeping in the chair like a baby. He was nothing except harmless and old. It seemed that the compassionate thing to do would be to let him stay put.

"See?" Window 4 continued. "It freaks us out to have him there. We'd ask José, but you're the only one here."

Then she walked away, which is what these tellers seemed to be doing right and left. Creating shipwrecks and then hopping into the lifeboat without me and rowing back to land.

I didn't quite know why this wasn't a job for security until I looked up and saw that Elizabeth Sabretta was checking her blood pressure, which she needs to do every day after she finishes lunch. I watched her roll up her sleeve and wrap the Velcro around her arm, then start her quick squeezing of the little black bag.

At that point I figured that asking an old guy to move was easier than what was going on in the doorway. I wasn't going to interrupt a woman in the middle of taking her own pulse. I would make myself equal to the task.

I straightened my tie and cuff links. I made my way over to the man in the chair. All the tellers were pretending to work but secretly looking at me out of the corner of their eyes. I looked the other way and forced myself to imagine this was not the case. They were not depending on me. I straightened the stanchions in the merchant line, and then I tiptoed over to the water fountain on my wafer soles. He was a tiny man, and the sweatsuit really hung on him. The visor covered almost all of his face.

I figured if I took a drink from the fountain, this would jog him awake, but it didn't do a thing for him. He was really out. I thought the sound of me or even the feel of my closeness, my shadow looming, might wake him. He was such a little gentleman. I could've picked him up with one hand.

I knelt at his elbow, but I didn't touch him right away. When I'm asleep, I hate that kind of invasion. "I'm sorry, sir," I said after a minute or so, nudging him a little. "We have to move you now."

I lifted the tennis visor and kind of peeked under it. How obvious is it that this was something I shouldn't have done? I swear I heard a sound when I did it, too. Like a car squealing tires, like wind whistling through barbed wire on an open barren plain.

It was all twisted up, the face. Frozen in a permanent expression. I snapped the fucking visor down. I glanced over at the tellers, and every single one was looking back at me intently. Like a herd of animals from across a field. Window 4 was just finishing up with a customer. "Have a nice day," she said.

This is when I heard the rustle behind me. The sound of padding bare feet. I felt the hand on my shoulder and thought, José, finally, the cocksucker. I turned, ready to punch him in the face, but when I looked up, she was there. The Woman I Used to Love. In the same torn nylon dress she was wearing that morning when I woke up next to her. She was smiling like an angel, dirty and wondrous. Except in this version of her, she had no teeth.

I put my hand on the man's shoulder and shook him. I took his pulse. Even if you don't know how to do it, you go through the motions. Like doctors on the medical shows.

Her hair was matted and she smelled like sulfur. Her smell was all around me.

"You know it's not appropriate to come here, Sally," I said. "This is where I work."

"Oh, honey," she said. "Oh, David." The Woman I Used to Love knelt beside me. She reached for the dead man's wallet, but I snatched it away before she could touch it.

"Please, Sally," I said. "You walked into the light, honey, remember? Please go back there. You look bad."

The Woman I Used to Love beamed and wavered. The inside of her mouth reminded me of a rabbit hole. "Oh, David," she said. "What a silly-willy."

I put my hand on the man's shoulder and shook him again. Again I took his pulse. Like I said, I didn't officially know how to do any of these things, but still I went through them. In Strawberry, New Mexico, I had done these things before. I put two fingers at the base of his throat and held them there. His skin was lukewarm, like tea going cold.

The Woman I Used to Love moved in closer to me. "David," she said, "where's Cynthia?"

If you think it's a problem that my dead wife is talking to me on a lunch hour, you would be absolutely correct.

I stood and turned toward the tellers. "Everyone get over here," I said. "I mean right, right now!"

The Woman I Used to Love crossed her bony arms. "Please, silly-willy," she said. "Tell me."

"Cynthia's not here, Sally," I said. "She's not with me anymore."

The Woman I Used to Love reached toward me. It was a hand, but not the kind you could touch. It felt like it had ahold of both my lungs.

"Don't be mad, Sally," I begged her. "Don't go."

But she did. She staggered toward the safe, and then she melted right into it. Through about seven layers of solid steel.

I can't account for much after that. It was like I was gradually being strangled. There were invisible forces choking off my air. My stomach was flopping around like a fish.

The other guy took over from there on out. I've introduced you to him before, right? The one who lives one day at a time and seems to know what to do?

This guy looked over at the tellers with authority. He spoke loudly, as if through a bullhorn. "We need to do something, for Christ's sake," he said. "The man is fucking dead."

Unlike during the earthquake, the tellers remained incredibly calm. It was like all the panicking that had gone on that morning for nothing had only been for José's benefit. I don't understand women at all.

"Jesus Christ," I heard the rational guy saying over and over again, and even he wasn't sounding all that rational. "Jesus fucking Christ."

Window 4 came over to me first, floating practically, like the man was still a living person. She appeared to be operating on a "show-me" basis, and it didn't seem like any of the other Windows were catching on to the reality, either.

"Did you hear me?" the functional guy said as loud as he could. "I'm not kidding. It's not a goddamn joke!"

This seemed to get the ball rolling. I felt a rush of femininity and soon was surrounded by a ring of concerned women.

Window 4 bent down beside me, and the ring tightened. She turned to me, her eyes wide, then reached out and touched my shoulder with her nail tips. If she'd pushed any harder, I would have fallen on my face. "What do we do?"

"Get his wallet out," I said. "Read it to me."

Window 4 did as she was told. "John Rivera," she said. "13842 El Circulo Drive." She looked up at the rest of the tellers. "Oh my God," she said.

Window 5, who is gentle and from Pakistan, reached for my hand. "I'm sorry, Mr. David," she said. "Mr. David, it wasn't your fault."

I blinked numbly at Window 5. Because what else do you do at that point? Tell the girl she's wrong? That she has no fucking idea how to do the math? She's underpaid enough around here, for God's sake. I looked deeply into the almost ridiculous purity of her eyes. "Get security," I said. "Call 911."

I stood up, and the ceiling and floor switched places. I'm not sure how quickly Elizabeth Sabretta got there. All I know is I heard cowboy boots, the tellers parted like a curtain, and she arrived in all the weaponry, the regalia, the pen flashlight, the windbreaker.

It was sickening how powerful she was up close, Elizabeth Sabretta. And no matter how I tried to uglify her, no matter how many harelips I gave her or withered hands, someone of her magnitude, someone who came in such a large dose, was never going to allow me anywhere near the Desdemona Room on a weeknight for a virgin cocktail. Not ever.

"What's happening here," Elizabeth Sabretta said to the general group. "What's going on?"

I tried to look at her, to respond to that question, but all I could do was look at John Rivera's stone-colored eyes, which were glaring upward, boring straight into the center of my brain.

"It's the guy who fell down," Window 4 said. "You remember, don't you? In the earthquake. He's dead."

Elizabeth Sabretta, for the first time I've ever seen her, did not know what to say. She scanned the faces of all the tellers. "José?"

"Cattlemen's," I said.

When she heard my voice, Elizabeth Sabretta turned and kept her eyes on me. It was like she was trying as hard as she was able to get every bit of information she could without speaking. "911?"

I nodded.

She looked down at John Rivera, then up at the tellers again. Her voice was very quiet. "Somebody go across the street."

Some clothing rustled, but nobody moved. Especially John Rivera.

"He either had a stroke," Window 4 announced, "or an aneurysm."

Elizabeth Sabretta seemed to be waiting for me to respond, but I couldn't confirm either of those diagnoses. Neither was a given. As I remembered, John Rivera falling over in his sweatsuit was like a sharp push from God.

Elizabeth Sabretta had her cell phone in her hand, but she didn't dial. Everyone was looking at John Rivera, who was lying there dead in the center of Modesto, in the center of the Bouquet Canyon Bank.

"Well, somebody has to do something," she said to Window 4, and when I heard her voice, a strange energy started to surge through my body. The energy of a living somebody, actually. Somebody in charge.

Without flinching, I slid my hands under John Rivera's

armpits and pulled him toward me. There was a gasp from the tellers as he fell forward out of the chair, but I caught him. I recognized this falling gesture by now, and I knew what to do. It was like catching a bag of rice. I have to be honest, he was lighter than the Woman I Used to Love when I lifted her from the bed. When I lifted her body and carried her out into the parking lot of the motel where we were staying in Strawberry, New Mexico, I got as far as our car, and it was like I wasn't carrying anything anymore. Once a person's gone, their real weight disappears.

So I picked up what was left of John Rivera, and I carried him over to the lending area. His arms dangled over my shoulders and bumped against my back. The tellers stayed in a whispering clump by the drinking fountain, while Elizabeth Sabretta followed right behind me, repeating commands in a quiet voice. "Don't drop him," she was saying. "Don't lose your balance. Don't crank his neck."

I laid him down on the love seat José put in front of my desk recently to encourage families and young couples to borrow. I told Elizabeth Sabretta to stick a cushion under his head, while I arranged his legs neatly in the sweatsuit. I slid the visor back down over his face.

It was weird what happened next, and I checked to see if she noticed it, but Elizabeth Sabretta still had her eyes on me. She didn't see John Rivera walk out of his own body like I did. He scuttled out of it like a hermit crab. She didn't see him jog on out through the walls of the bank and enter the desert of the central valley. The central valley that is a ghost of an ocean itself. John Rivera was on his way even farther west, moving at a good clip across the parking strip toward Cattlemen's and the RV dealership. Then into the soy fields. Disappearing down a long row into the haze.

"Hey," Elizabeth Sabretta said, shaking me a little. "Hey, I'm serious. Are you all right?"

"No" was definitely the answer to that question, but I turned to Elizabeth Sabretta and held back a response. Because how do I explain the dilemma of what I see to this woman? How do I explain that looking at her is like an overdose? And that being kept away from her is also a similar kind of ecstasy?

How do I tell her? How? In not so many words. How one night I will drive to the Desdemona Room uninvited. How I will walk into the bar like anybody else and take a seat on the closest available stool. How I will look the same as every man there, the only difference is that I will be yellow and have giant floppy ears. Elizabeth Sabretta will be working the floor in a short skirt and form-fitting top. No walkie-talkie. No cell phone. No gun. She will approach me and raise an eyebrow, smile.

"Hi, bunny," she will say. "You look thirsty."

Her face will be warm and full of makeup. She will bring me ice water for hours, until everyone has gone home and it's time to turn on the overhead lights. Then the bartender will start the vacuum cleaner, and Elizabeth Sabretta will come out from the back room in her street clothes and crawl into my lap.

"You don't have to worry," I will say, wrapping my large furry paws around her. I'm just a bunny with a dead wife and a kid who's a ward of the state, and Elizabeth Sabretta will laugh and laugh while I tickle her.

"Get away from me, you crazy," she'll say, cuddling closer. "David, I mean it. You're a rabbit, all right? Get away."

I looked at Elizabeth Sabretta and swallowed. I drank in her closeness like booze. "Go ahead and sit down," I said, and she lowered herself into one of the chairs. "Are you sure you're okay?"

Elizabeth Sabretta shrugged and gestured toward the body. "Jesus. I don't know," she said. "How are you?"

I couldn't really say it, but I think I was happy right then. In perfect control of my mind and motor skills. It was peaceful, frankly, just us two in the mini–living room, with John Rivera lying there in between. For a minute we were like a family, but Elizabeth Sabretta wasn't able to recognize it. Elizabeth Sabretta thinks she's the only one with a sad story. She thinks she's the only one to ever die from grief and still be up walking around.

"Why are you looking at me like that?" she said. "What's wrong?"

But what on earth could my answer possibly have been? Right then the lending area felt like our own private meadow. At that moment we could have been two of the luckiest bunnies in the world.

"There's nothing wrong with me," I said. "You've been a great help. Why don't you go outside and wait for the ambulance now. Go ahead."

Elizabeth Sabretta raised her head to look at me. "Are you sure?" she said, and I told her I was. I touched her shoulder for reassurance. I even smiled.

And as the loan officer watches the security guard collapse into the arms of his newly arrived boss and the two Nordic-looking paramedics, I know what you're thinking. I'm thinking it, too, as real as if it's already happening.

You think: Here's a guy standing alone near his desk with a bottle of DayQuil in his pocket while sirens go off. Here's a picture of him walking out into the sun, popping the childproof cap, and taking the whole thing practically in one swallow. The world is murmuring alternatives, of course, but he's only savoring the fall. Slipping through the glass walls of the Bouquet Canyon Bank. Walking step by step out into the parking strip, drinking the cold medicine that is bright as human blood.

BIG CATS

T his summer," Polly says to me in her soft, scratchy-gravel voice, "I'm making it with a forklifter."

We're sitting alone, the two of us, in the woods behind our development, the Sylvan Townhouse Estates, changing into work uniforms, and her whispering mouth is up so close to my earlobe I can feel her lip gloss.

"Don't pair off with Polly all the time," my mother keeps on begging. "You need to expand your horizons." But she doesn't see that Polly is my horizon, and when she puts her arm around my shoulder and squeezes, the sweet, oily smell of her bubble gum makes me picture a hot tropical place where the two of us are getting stared at through the palm trees by hundreds of eyes.

"Last summer was for wishing," Polly says. "This summer is for fucking."

Her words are invisible, but they crash between my legs like giant cymbals.

Yesterday all the second-season girls with work permits marked age fourteen were taken aside at the orientation by Division Manager Weiss of the Washington Park Zoo. We were lined up on the loading dock at the side entrance after he had all the boys go stand by the time clock outside his office, and he told us: "No female food and giftshop concessionaires are to mix with warehouse personnel on zoo grounds in zoo uniforms, no matter what."

"Now, ladies," he said, leaning his bubble rear up against one of those oxygen tanks they use for pop, "warehouse jobs at these zoological gardens are community-service positions, and the policy here is to leave those gentlemen well enough alone, especially while the Elephant House is under construction."

"Picture the Weiss fingering his vagina," Polly said out of the side of her mouth, and I was about to fall over on the floor holding my stomach. The things Polly says can make me do that. She makes me fall down in public all the time.

Now Polly scoots away, and dewy pine needles cling to the back of her legs. "Say it, Brenda," she says, "that's an order," so I take off my summer shorts, and in my newest bikini underwear with the leopard thunderbolt, I do as I am told, shouting it out to her and the dark, empty woods: "We fuck something from the warehouse or nothing at all!"

Last summer, when we were new, we couldn't believe the boys. Eight boys working Main Cafeteria, five boys with money belts taking tickets for the boats and trains, six boys in white paper hats leaning up against shade trees selling popcorn and Sno-Kones, three garbage pickers. But the forklifters were actual men. Sweaty, shirtless, numberless men with skull wristbands and visors and tattoos, racing in and out of the scaffolding behind the broken-down Elephant House, backing boxes full of things into dark doorways, shifting gear after jerky gear.

"That's right, blood sister," Polly says, lifting up her hand. I lift mine, too, and we clap those hands together hard. In the air they are the same hand. We leave them there and intertwine fingers. *Yeah.*

We have to be at work in less than twenty minutes, but Polly doesn't seem to be in a hurry at all. She's lying topless in the moss with her eyes closed, humming a song she's making up right this second, and I know for certain she's got a much better chance than I do of making it with forklifters. She has nice wide hips compared to me, and soft thighs that don't spread out when she sits on fences. Polly's hair is towhead also, and so frizzy she can even use an Afro comb on it, no matter the style.

All I've got is plain silky brown hair that wants to lay down and not do a single thing. "It wants to be auburn, too," my mother says, but she won't take me to the colorist until I'm fifteen. My hips are not wide, either, but narrow, like a giraffe's.

The only thing in the entire world I do have, compared to Polly Swann, though, is a chest.

Even to this day she doesn't need to wear a bra under her uniform or any of her other clothes, and looking at her now, at her bare-boy flatness on top, makes me worry all of a sudden that they will never grow and she will end up being bottom-heavy. But then I remember that both of us have pretty decent faces, and if you took the bottom of her body and my top and put them together, I think forklifters would like us. I think we would balance each other out.

That's all I'm thinking about when I'm looking at her, regular thoughts, but a cloud comes over Polly's face. "What are you staring at?" she says, covering her nipples with her palms, which is easy because they are only about the size of two pink pennies.

"Nothing, blood sister," I tell her, raising up my shirt and giving her a quick flash of my mother's bra with the lace cross straps and the rose in the center. "I stole it from her drawer."

"No point when it's too big."

"Not for long," I say, showing her the safety pin I used to clip the back. "Almost."

"That is disgusting, Brenda," Polly says, scrunching up her face and rolling away. "Old sick-lady clothes."

I whip a stick in her direction. "She's not sick."

"Whatever."

"Well," I say in a high, stupid voice, knowing by the tone that I will live to regret it, "can't go braless anymore, like you."

Polly shoves her middle finger in my direction. "Fuck off, anyway," she says, grabbing her clothes up in a wad. "I'm not sitting around here so you can stare at me like a perv."

Then she turns her back and slips into the rest of her zoo uniform, which is brown shirt with official patch, brown knee-length tie apron, and ironed cotton pants with a crease. No jeans.

Neither of us says anything while we're dressing, and when she's done, Polly leans up against a peeling birch whose papery bark crinkles as she rips big sheets of it away. I know she shouldn't do that to the tree, but I'm scared to say anything, even when there's a smooth naked patch on the trunk that looks like it hurts.

"I'm not mad anyway, freak," she says, grabbing the big kitchen mitt we keep in our hiding place near the fence. "You just shouldn't get so excited."

"Oh, please," I tell her, reaching for the pot holder, which in reality is mine because I stole it from my mother after the hysterectomy last summer. In the old days before she had everything removed, she would have missed that thing, but now that she's on the different hormones, she barely ever cooks anymore. If it wasn't for Ed the Renter who lives in the downstairs and takes care of her, she'd probably set her bathrobe on fire.

"Get going then, Brennie," Polly says, shoving the pot holder on my hand, and I lift the bottom strand of barbed wire so she can slide under. When it's my turn, I hear one of the peacocks calling down in the zoo, and it makes me feel eerie. Like the sign of death.

"Brush me off?" I say, turning my back to Polly, but she's already balancing along the tracks of the little kid's railroad, heading off.

"I'm going my special way, okay?" she says, adjusting her Afro comb, and even though I want to, I don't follow her or try to catch up. Instead I act like I've got other things I'm thinking about, and my own path, too. She turns left at the Arctic Wolves without even looking around, so I cut up the other way by the Sun Bears on purpose, because that's the way it is with Polly. You have to give her space to do things. Like when we're at Crystal Ship getting records, or at the Brass Plum Boutique, I let her browse on her own. I don't follow her from rack to rack when we're shopping and talk about the things she's looking at. And if you do that, if you ignore her, she'll always come back to you and show you the things she's picking.

I know Polly's special route to Main Cafeteria is shorter and she's secretly trying to beat me, so I jet past the Hippo Pond, sprint around the Ladybug Theater, and cut up through Mini-Everglades. There's nobody around, so I pretend to be a spy on a mission. I hit the tunnel behind Polar Bear Island at my fastest pace yet, until I see a fat fire hose snaking along the ground toward the side entrance, and I have to stop then because I know it leads to a zookeeper.

The only reason I ever wanted us to work at the zoo at all was because of the animals. In the newspaper, when I showed the ad to Polly, it said, *Animal Lovers Wanted.* But zoo policy is that no one is allowed to assist the zookeepers. You can't touch the food or help or even go into the Nocturnal or Monkey Houses when they're being cleaned. Weiss says you cannot ever plug things in for a zookeeper either or help them screw in a hose because there could be a lawsuit.

"Leave the keepers officially alone" was how he put it. "They *are* this zoo, and they don't have time to talk with any of the food and beverage personnel."

Zookeepers always come to work in perfect security-guard-looking uniforms with fancy walkie-talkies and rings of keys. Except it's not like you'd imagine from the nature shows where zoo experts are always so excited to show people animals and baby animals and how to hold them and things. It's rare to ever see the same zookeeper twice in one day. The only ones we see a lot are the two women who get to take care of the lions and tigers and snow leopards. "Big Cat Lesbians," Polly calls them, but I don't think they sleep in the same bed. Last summer we saw them be in the same cage, practically, with a cougar.

I run my hand along the railing of Polar Bear Island as I sneak beside the hose watching Uba, the mother polar bear, and Eka, the baby, while a zookeeper in work gloves and rubber boots stands right below the fake iceberg where they are sleeping, hosing down what's supposed to be the Arctic Ocean.

She is tall and muscley, with strawberry-blond dreadlocks spiking out through the back of her baseball cap, and she's sending a river of thick green water into a drain hole. There's a radio on down in the den too, tuned to "Jamaica Sounds" on KISN. The music is up pretty loud, and her back is to me, so I quickly bend down and just for a minute touch the hose, because I've heard they can handle a lot of pressure. Jim Kemper, one of the high school rehires, says they can take up to forty pounds per square inch.

I've still got my hands on the hose when the water stops, and when I look up, she is staring across her shiny blue surface of painted waves.

"Can I help you, my girl?" she says loudly over the radio, and I can't tell if she's upset or not because her eyes are covered with little round sunglasses like John Lennon's.

"Sorry," I say, removing my hand from that hose and standing up to walk away. But instead of getting mad, the zookeeper smiles kind of crookedly. She goes over and turns down the volume on her radio so it's just dim mumbling, then comes over to the den doorway, dragging the heavy hose behind her like it's a body.

"What can I do for you today?" she says, still smiling, and I see there's a little chip in one of her front teeth.

I peek over her shoulder at Uba and Eka to see if they're listening to any of this, but those bears are lying flat on their faces like they're dead.

And even though I know we're never supposed to speak, I look her straight in the eye, just like Polly would have, and ask her the question we've had ever since the beginning of last summer when we saw the male snow leopard on top of the female, making love to her over and over again on a sawed-off log.

"I heard all the animals here are on birth-control pills," I say. "Is that correct?"

The keeper doesn't answer right away. Instead she takes off her sunglasses and looks at me seriously, checking out my uniform, and I can tell she thinks it was a smart question. "You betcha," she says. "But only the females, my girl."

The first thing I see when I get to Weiss's office in back of the gift shop is a bunch of first-season hires standing around in a little huddle in the courtyard with their plastic orientation notebooks and fold-out food-service maps. The pants they are wearing are way too dressy, of course, and they'll be sorry if Weiss puts any of them on french-fry grill.

I waltz through the center of the new-hire clump without having to say excuse me, then head for the second-season area, where I see Polly in a group of rehire boys, leaning back against the wall with Doug Sengstake and Eric Folkstad, talking. At first she looks over and doesn't say anything to me, so I roll up my uniform sleeves and check the pockets of my cotton pants, until I hear Polly give a squealy little scream.

"Blood sister," she calls to me now, because Sengstake has grabbed her around the waist, and Folkstad is reaching his whole hand up her apron.

"Blood sister," Polly yells again, trying to stomp on Folkstad's toes to keep him away. "C'mere and help me, honey, please." And even though I think technically we're still supposed to be mad at each other, I elbow in as close as I can through all the other rehire boys who are starting to cluster around.

"I'm coming, Poll," I say, but five of them grab my arms behind my back, and all I can do is thrash while everybody starts rooting for people: boys for Sengstake, girls for Polly and me, until there's a muffled knocking from inside Weiss's Plexiglas and everybody gets quiet. All except for Polly, who's fighting so hard she doesn't even hear the door to the office complex creak its way open.

"Let *go*, faggot," she screams, pony-kicking out fast and sharp at Sengstake's shins. "Butt soldier!"

"Mademoiselle Swann," Weiss says in his calm dictator voice, and as she turns, all the wild electricity in her eyes fades. "Shall we have a little rendezvous in my office?"

Polly's mouth works up and down, as if her jawbone is out of whack. "They're the ones who started it," she says, waving in the boys' direction. "Tell him, Brenda."

"She didn't do it," I say, looking down at Weiss's Nikes. "It was two ganging up on one."

Weiss turns to me, smiling with his mouth but not with his eyes. "Mademoiselle Hopkins," he says to me. "Your friend has violated a very important rule. My staff does not use profanity. That's not how I run a zoo."

You don't run a zoo at all is what I want to tell his fake French face. *You are not the one with reggae hair and a hose in the Polar Bear Display. You are not in a special uniform with your partner, practically inside the cage with a cougar.*

But Weiss doesn't care what anybody thinks. "Patch not showing," he says, pointing to my rolled-up sleeve in front of the new hires. "Now, let's get inside for day assignments, troops."

As soon as Weiss and Polly are gone, all the boys crowd in around the assignment sheet so nobody else can see it. Half those boys get garbage duty anyway, which is so easy. Girls don't ever get to do garbage. When it's finally my turn, I skip my name and look for Polly's first. *Swann, Polly*, it says, *Troubleshooter*, which is nothing less than a total jail sentence: stocking straws and napkins inside the Solarium and busing the tables on the Picnic Deck with all the yellow jackets swirling around your hands.

I follow my finger up the list and find my name in Weiss's curly writing just as Polly gets back from her lecture. Her face is soft, and her blur of hair looks like it's been scribbled around her head with a crazy white crayon. She brushes by me like we're strangers and goes up to the corkboard, running her sky blue fingernail up and down the assignments until she gets to her name, then mine: *Hopkins, Brenda: Big Cats Candy Kiosk*.

Considering how amazing that day assignment is compared to hers, I expect her to snub me like before, but instead she treats me fake-nice, the way the runner-up girl at a beauty contest would treat the girl who won.

"Hey, Big Cats Candy Kiosk," she says, giving me the kind of excited hug that doesn't mean anything. "Congrats, baby. Con-grats."

"You can have it, I promise," I say. "We can trade."

"Don't worry, kitten," she says without meeting my eyes. "Nothing Mama can't handle."

"What about the Weiss, though?" I ask, and Polly sighs.

"Weiss is so gay, Brenda," she says, turning to the time clock and thwonking her card down into the machine's loud teeth. "What else do you need to know, or anyone?"

What every member of the food and gift personnel knows is that Big Cats Candy Kiosk is the best assignment in the entire zoo. It's built right in the middle of the Central Concourse and looks like a little round temple from China. The whole front of it is Plexiglas, for one thing, and gives you an excellent view of the Big Cats outdoor exhibit, which is shaped like a giant pie. Lions, snow leopards, cougars, and jaguars split it in quarters, and from the Candy Kiosk you can see right into the sector that looks like a real African semi-desert. The only things separating you from the lion and lionesses are a walkway, a moat, a low hedge, and a railing.

In Big Cats Kiosk, Weiss has the candy organized on a lower shelf in his own order, like library books; plus, you have your own phone and authorized permission to call forklifters if you run out of any brand.

As soon as I get to Big Cats, I check my inventory, then call my mother. I've told her that using an outside phone line is against Weiss's policy, but she still says to do it anyway. "It gives me something to look forward to" is what she tells me, even though it takes her more than ten rings sometimes to get to the phone.

Today she picks up right away, though, which means she probably still has it with her in the bed. "Oh hi, BeeBee," she says in her sleepy underwater voice. "What are you doing?"

I'm about to tell her "Working" or "Selling stuff," which is what I always say, except right then I see that same zookeeper from the morning, driving slowly up the concourse in one of the official green zoo pickups.

"Nothing," I say, twisting the phone cord around my fingers as that zookeeper comes right up alongside my kiosk and leaves her truck idling. "Just feeding lions is all. Sometimes other animals. Going into their cages, too."

"Oh," my mother says. "That sounds like fun. Is Polly with you?"

I watch as the zookeeper takes a king-size Shop-Vac out of the back of her truck and carries it around toward the side entrance to Big Cats. "Are you making any other friends?" my mother says, but before I can answer, a big senior-citizen group arrives along the concourse and starts blocking my view of the entire semi-desert. They are teetering down the steep hill from the entrance in a zigzag pattern and have balloons tied to their wheelchairs and walkers. Senior citizens and the people who take care of them hardly ever want candy, but still, I feel dread, especially when I see Polly strolling along behind some of the stragglers.

"I have to go," I say, but my mother is so slow on the uptake.

"What's going on, BeeBee?" she says. "Are you mad?"

"I'm not," I say. "I am not mad," but of course she won't believe me, and as I hang up, I can still hear her in a half-panic, calling my name.

At first Polly almost passes me by with the senior citizens, then at the last second, she turns and stares at both me and Big Cats Candy Kiosk, as if she's never been more surprised. The green zookeeper's truck is still idling out there, too, right in front of her face, but she doesn't act like she's noticed.

"Oh, Brennie, it's you," she says, putting her face up to the hole in the Plexiglas with a giant smile. "I couldn't remember where you were."

"Female animals here are on the pill," I tell her the minute I let her in the door, and finally, Polly looks out at the green pickup and narrows her eyes.

"You're so full of shit, Brenda," she says. "Who told you, anyway? Her?"

"That's correct." And then I tell Polly every single detail while we split a Twix and suck the chocolate off our fingers. About Uba and Eka and the smell of the water. The chip in her tooth and the UB40 on the radio. Her dreads.

When I'm done, Polly looks at me and sighs. "All that's very sweet," she says, tracing her initials in the dust on the window. "Are you in love now, blood sister?"

"Shut up."

Polly swings her legs, and I try and ignore the bang of her high-tops on my clean cabinets. "Well, I found a rat in the grease bucket, is what I'd like you to know," she says. "Weiss had me call forklifters."

I look at Polly, and my stomach feels like it's diving way down. "So?"

Polly picks up a box of Hot Tamales and taps them against her knee. "Brenda, Brenda, Brenda," she says in a way that makes me hate the sound of my own name. "My point is, I made contact with the warehouse, which is more than I can say for you."

I inform her that I am, in my own way, making forklifter contact, and she can go finger herself, but Queen Polly only shakes her head grandly.

"Maybe I'm meeting someone later, blood sister," she says. "Which is more than I can say for you."

"What's that supposed to mean?"

"Oh, I don't know," Polly says, brushing off the back of her pants. "It's hard to say."

"It isn't that hard," I tell her, "just open your mouth," but instead of answering, all Polly has to do is stand there and I can see it inside her. The glow. That same green nuclear power she inherited from her mother, Leanne Swann, who, last time Polly talked about it, was dating a tennis pro from Corno's Produce and having an abortion.

I'll screw a forklifter right now, I want to promise Polly. *Yes, I definitely will.* But then I think of Leanne Swann in her two-piece tennis outfit, compared to my mother in her wilty bathrobe, and I can see why Polly would doubt me.

"Move aside," I say to her, reaching for the phone. "What's the number of the forklifters?"

"You know it, Hopkins," she says with her victory smirk. "Dial it yourself."

The forklifters take an even longer time to pick up than my mother does, and when they finally do, all I hear is a roaring from a giant machine, like some kind of shredder.

"Warehouse," the voice says, and my ribs close up.

"Pick up on deck," somebody else yells in the background.

"Warehouse," the forklifter says again, louder, and when I hear the engines revving behind him, I can't help but picture us together in the crooked scaffolding of the Elephant House, doing it in the different positions of sex Polly and I saw in the *Dutch Book of Eros:* sometimes in front of an audience, wearing girdles and open tuxedos; sometimes just alone, with neckties and strapped-on extra penises.

"Warehouse," I hear again, and my tongue turns so icy hot in my mouth I can't move it.

"Help me," I mouth to Polly, covering the receiver, but instead she grabs the phone.

"Yes, this is Brenda Hopkins over at Big Cats Candy Kiosk," she says officially into the receiver. "Would it be possible to suck my pussy?"

"Shut up!" I scream, wrestling the phone away and shoving her out the door, but it doesn't do any good, because in a minute I see the same evil, fluffy head pass by in front of my window. I cover the mouth hole of my Plexiglas, but I can still feel her breath on my palm.

"Gotcha," she says.

Then, right in front of me, while she knows I'm watching, she runs her finger along the side of the zookeeper's green truck. There isn't anybody around to see her, so she does it slow, making sure I see the line her finger is leaving across the dusty paint. She circles the whole truck like that, with her finger dragging, then jumps up on the back bumper and swings herself aboard.

I pound the window with my fist, but she ignores me and walks all around inside the open back of that zookeeper's truck, touching and stepping over everything she sees, the rolled-up hose and the handles of other weird official-looking animal equipment, even though that zookeeper could come out at any time and catch her.

"You better knock it off," I hiss at her through the Plexiglas hole, but she knows I am trapped in here, in my kiosk. She knows if a customer comes to buy candy in an empty kiosk, Weiss would fire me on the spot.

I drop my forehead onto the counter and stare down at the rows of candy. I even take a complete inventory again, until I notice Polly stop and lift that zookeeper's radio over her head. She holds it up there for a long time to make sure I've seen it, then lowers it next to her face and pretends to scream, as if it's a prize she's just won on a game show. The truck heaves as she jumps up and down with the radio, and I can't believe this is happening. I can't believe I have called her sister, that blood from our fingertips has ever even mixed.

I check up and down the concourse for candy customers, Weiss, or forklifters coming to suck pussy, but thank God, none of them are coming.

And by now Polly has on the zookeeper's hat and is making out with the radio, pretending to tongue-kiss the front of it. She stops, pointing at me from the truck, and it is obvious what she is saying: "Big Cat Lez-bo. You You You. "

I hold my middle finger up to the window, but Polly, slowly, slowly, with a wild orgasmic look on her face, takes hold of the radio by the cord and starts lowering it down her body, inch by inch into the cab of the truck. While she does that, she starts to dance, a seriously sexy dance, as if she's trying out to be a stripper, and even though it's the most embarrassing, shittiest thing, of course she looks good. She looks good doing it.

I cover my face with the clipboard, but it's impossible to do that for very long. There's nowhere else to look but back at Polly. She lifts one hand over her head and pretends to twirl a lasso. The other hand she puts between her legs, then looks at me and swings her hips, pretending to be the zookeeper. "Oh my God, Brenda," she calls, lifting up her shirt. "I'm so gay for you."

At Polly's townhouse, she and Leanne Swann swap clothes and scarves. They put lipstick on each other like they are Greek sisters from a sorority. I've seen them trade things, use tampons out of the same box, whisper to each other like they are the only ones in the entire world. "This is my baby," Leanne will say about Polly, as if I'm not even in the room. "Gorgeous, right? She's my best friend."

The door of my kiosk explodes in front of me, and when I burst out onto the concourse with my inventory clipboard, the whole world feels like it's at a slant.

"You better fucking cut it out, Swann," I warn her from across the walkway, lifting the clipboard, but she only laughs and starts to go at it even harder.

"Oh God, girlfriend," she says, rubbing the radio across her chest. "Nobody does it like you."

"Quit!" I say, grabbing for the radio, but Polly is still dancing away.

"Oh yeah?" she says in a voice like syrup. "And who's gonna stop me? *Dyke!*"

I draw my arm back, aiming for her mouth, and the clipboard slices through the air just like the boomerangs they have hanging on the walls in the Koala Kabin, whistling past her head, over the truck, across the fat hedge, and right into the middle of the semi-desert.

Polly drops the radio with a clank, and I run to the railing and see my clipboard in the long grass, lying about fifteen feet away from three lionesses, who all look up at me with golden eyes and blink.

"Nice job," Polly says. "Stupid."

Slowly, I turn to the truck with a heat around me that is more than just burning.

"I'm real sorry about that," says Polly, pointing down into the display. "Maybe you better call your mama."

I look up at her face, but the sun is too bright. A white ring around a world of rampaging fire. I ask her if maybe she'd like to repeat that.

"Oh yes," says my friend Polly. "Absolutely. I said call your mama, BeeBee. Your poor, sad, dried-up mama."

"What did you say?"

"You heard me. *Hysterectomy.*"

My eyes tear wide open to take her in and for the first time since I ever saw her, I can picture Polly Swann's dead skeleton lying in her grave. I lean forward, and my voice feels so velvety and viper-quiet I think it might be coming from the mouth of one of the reptiles. "You stupid, titless bitch," I whisper. "*Slut.*"

She springs from the truck like it's a trampoline, and we are on the cement then, joined. I can't believe how easy it is to hit her. My fists drop down and down like carpet bombs. It doesn't seem to hurt when she's hitting me, either, and we roll back and forth on the cement like pit wrestlers.

She goes for the pocket of my apron, and when I hear the rip, I grab for the zoo patch on her arm. There is a giant stretch, the sound of material giving way, and then I choke her until her face purples out.

I press my forehead onto hers, and I want to hate-kiss her over and over and smash her teeth. My lips are inches from her lips.

"Pill popper's baby," she rasps, digging at my chest for my mother's bra. "Sterile!" And as she gets hold of it, yanking the straps, I remember suddenly what it is my mother said, and I sink my fingers deep into the mass of cotton-white hair. "Leanne Swann is a two-dollar whore," I say, wagging her head back and forth in my hands. *"Abortion!"*

All at once there are words, then footsteps, and my hold on Polly feels like its loosening. I reach out to hit as hard as I can at the thing between us, but I am being pressed into the ground by a cool gray shadow that blots out the sun.

"My patch, she took my patch," a hoarse voice is shouting, and when I open my eyes, I am on my back somehow and the sound is Polly, practically crying like I have never seen her before, holding the place on her uniform where her zoo patch used to be. I follow the finger she is pointing at me and see that it leads to my hand, where crazy threads are poking out through the fist.

"It's all right now," a voice is saying. "Let's everybody calm way the hell down."

On my chest there is a tapping, and when I look there, I see it's the knotted end of a reddish dreadlock dangling in front of my eyes like the tip of a paintbrush. Then I know exactly where I am.

"Are you hurt?" she says to me. "Can you get up?" It's a nice voice, smooth and deep and faraway.

"You're going to fire us, aren't you?" I say.

"Oh no she isn't!" Polly says, as if she's about to have some kind of tantrum. "I cannot be fired. I can-not!"

The zookeeper turns to Polly. "I need it quiet from you now," she says, in a much rougher voice than she used on me. "I don't want to hear another word."

Polly's mouth snaps shut with enough force to bite off her tongue. I have never seen her clam up like that, not ever.

"I'm definitely hurt," I say. "I might be paralyzed."

"Uh-huh. Let's get you on your feet."

Her smell is like hay and cigarettes, and I put my whole weight into her arms. I could not do that to my mother, but all this zookeeper does is hoist me right up.

"I'm sorry to interrupt," Polly says, taking a step forward and tapping the zookeeper on the shoulder, "but an inventory clipboard is in with your lions. She threw it at me. She totally attacked me with it, and it flew in."

"She was in your truck first," I say as calmly as I can. "She was in the back, touching your equipment and doing a striptease."

The zookeeper holds up a work glove. "I'm not interested," she says. "Can you girls settle this now, or do you need inter-vention?"

Polly and I look at each other, but as soon as our eyes come together, they jump apart like the wrong ends of magnets.

I toss the patch to Polly, but she lets it flutter down on top of her tennis shoes.

"I'll take that as a yes," the zookeeper says. "Am I right?"

Polly brushes off her pant legs. There is gravel in her hair, and red crescent moon marks are on her cheeks from my fingernails. It looks as if she just got raped.

"All right, then, girls," the zookeeper says. "I'm going in for this damn clipboard. You two stay right here."

And before either of us can argue, that zookeeper hefts the Shop-Vac into the back of her green truck, kills the engine, and strides off toward the side entrance.

Neither of us says anything to the other one. We just wander toward the railing, as quiet and stunned-seeming as the animals. There is no sound either, except for the baboons, who are always screeching twenty-four hours a day anyway with their fangs out and their swollen red bottoms.

Inside the display, on top of their grassy cement hill, the three lionesses are still lying side by side, taking turns licking each other's paws and ears. Every so often they swish their tails at the lion too, who is relaxing on a flat rock not far away, watching the women in his pride clean themselves with their rough tongues. And in between the two groups, lying upside down at the edge of the central watering hole, is my inventory clipboard, looking ridiculous in there, like some weird commercial is being made about office supplies.

"Jesus, look," Polly whispers, but she doesn't need to open her mouth, because I can see that zookeeper fine by myself, bending down through the low cave opening at the back of the display that's spray-painted with running herds of wildebeests. Her hands are quiet at her sides, and she comes out slowly with total expertise, like she doesn't want to make any rapid moves.

"Oh my God," Polly says as the zookeeper rises from her

crouch and moves out into the pen, as if it is not just tan cement she's walking on but deep Serengeti sand.

"We need to be quiet and calm," I say to Polly. "They could tear her up."

But as the zookeeper's safari boots rustle through the dry grass, her confidence is so complete that the lionesses lie right where they are, yawning and blinking, and the lion just goes on shaking the bugs out of his mane, like this kind of unbelievable thing happens all the time.

In less than a minute, that zookeeper is exactly where she needs to be. She bends down like a karate fighter, straddling the water hole, and when she has a hold on the clipboard, she looks up at me directly, with that same crooked smile from the morning, and winks before lifting my candy inventory up over her head and carrying it at the exact same pace back out through the door.

There is a short silence after she disappears when I can hear only my heart and Polly's breath as she leans against me whispering, "Holy shit."

Then somebody starts to clap. I snap my head around and there they all are, the exact same group of senior citizens, back now, I guess, from Primates. They have all wheeled up behind one old man with binoculars, who is focusing on the door the zookeeper just used to exit. "That was my clipboard," I say to him, and he smiles at all of us with very white and young-looking teeth.

"Congratulations, young lady," he says. "Bravissima."

And when they hear him say that, the rest of the seniors clap even harder. They just keep on clapping and clapping and staring into the semi-desert with their balloons bobbing until Polly and I both do the same.

And while I clap, I picture what we all must look like there, and my whole body gets really big from the awe, until I am a giant, standing over the zoo in a tight silver uniform that is the exact same color as the clouds. And looking down, I see the whole green field across from the Jazz Concert Bandshell, and it is shining like a bright neon square, filled with every single forklifter who works here, all staring up at my hugeness, all hoping to screw me.

Then I get even bigger still, until I can see right down into our townhouse, where my mother is floating in the air, six feet at least, above our couch. "Look at me, BeeBee," she says. "I'm flying."

And way down below me, tiny munchkin Polly is squinting up, cupping her hands around her mouth, saying I'm still her blood sister. She promises I am. And I smile down at my friend then, from that great height. I smile almost gently, because I know that if I wanted to, I could lift her into the sun.

GOLDEN PIONEERS

Their story begins in 1963, in the parking lot of a small plasterboard motel. The place can be easy to miss, tucked away at the edge of the railroad yards where the Salem City Center on-ramp meets Interstate 5. Next door there's a chicken restaurant that's struggling to stay in business, and beyond that, the long dark hill of Salem proper, where all the houses and their people are at rest tonight under the eternal gaze of the Golden Pioneer, who stands astride the Oregon State Capitol Building with his eyes on the future and his fist in the air.

In spite of its humble surroundings, there is a charm about this roadside inn. Each of its white bungalows has been freshly painted, and little blue anchors hang at jaunty angles on every door. Captain Johnson's Oceanside it's called, though Salem is over eighty miles from the sea.

The neon sign that recommends Captain Johnson's to passing drivers on the freeway is more cheerful than most, and it pulses its red and blue beacon (namely a winking seagull in a tilted sailor's cap) out across the four-lane highway and up into the darker universe with powerful hypnotic confidence.

This evening the sign has not yet succeeded at seducing the distant ocean inland, but it has managed to lure a rusted-out VW Karmann Ghia, which idles, pops, and backfires outside the motel's tiny office.

Behind the desk, the proprietor sits in quiet contemplation of the FBI's Ten Most Wanted list, prominently displayed on the fraying corkboard above the rotary telephone. At the moment, the man is captivated by the smiling face of one Bierelane Leonard, an armed robber and mass murderer, and gives little regard to the young couple from the local college who are watching him carefully through the front windshield of the VW. So well meaning and young and achingly fallible, these two. I'd like to tell you they're meant for each other.

The young man is at the wheel with the heat on, the radio. He's taking several moments to go over the falsehoods regarding age and marital status that he will soon attempt to pass over on the owner of the Captain Johnson's, once the man is finished with the hardened criminals and moves on to the harmless liars.

He's dressed up for a night out, this young man, but even so I can pick him out of a crowd, can recognize him as a nineteen-year-old version of my father. Scrubbed, crew-cutted, white-socked, chinoed. He's looking his best tonight, listening to the Shirelles sing "Foolish Little Girl."

The only problem is his white button-down shirt with the pink spatters of frog's blood on it from the morning's dissection in biology class. (He had no idea the insides of the thing would squirt up that way!) But right now he is less concerned about the stain than the girl sitting next to him who is about to become my mother. How will she feel about the crooked cuffs of his pants once he gets her in a room and they begin to undress under the light?

His own mother, Priscilla, used to hem his pants for him,

but she died last year from a nerve disease no one could explain. When the doctors talked about it, their eyes would wander away. He remembers what they looked like perfectly, their sharp cheekbones and noses, their starched white coats and expensive leather shoes. He remembers these things more than anything they actually said, except that Priscilla would kill herself if she didn't stop smoking. Her cigarettes are still in his father's freezer. Three cartons of Newports on the left-side front, stacked end to end and furry with frost. He inherited her sewing box, and he takes care of his own cuffs now.

My father wipes a sweaty palm down the front of his raincoat, and the girl beside him comes to the rescue immediately. In earnest.

"I could do it, you know," she says. "If you want to stay here. If you're—"

As far as she is aware, she did not actually say the word "scared," but as my father slams the car door and starts tearing across the parking lot away from her, she isn't quite sure.

Lately, she has had a terrible habit of not knowing whether she was just thinking about a word or actually saying it out loud. The weekend before last, when she visited her parents up in Portland, for example, an air-raid siren went off at six o'clock in the morning, and as part of a practice evacuation in preparation for a nuclear holocaust, she and her parents were forced to drive with coats on over their pajamas down the old Columbia Gorge Highway going five miles an hour in a chain of traffic as far as she cared to look in either direction to an assigned bomb shelter dug out of the side of a hill in St. Helen's. And when her father put her in charge of the thermal blankets and the box of canned food, she thought she said to him, "Sure, Daddy."

She knew she did. But her father, who was from a small impassable slope of ground in Scotland, and whom, throughout the course of her life, she had seen smile approximately twice, walked up to her and stood with his face right in her face, his expression frigid with rage.

"Everyone here is trying to save themselves, Mary," he said. "Do you think it's funny to play deaf and dumb?"

My mother turns up the Shirelles and smooths the hem of her skirt over her kneecaps. Had she done the same thing with her date just now, too? She decides to try not to remember. Whatever is happening to her in the present will probably sort itself out somewhere along the line.

Without stopping to catch his breath, my father arrives in the motel lobby, ready to launch into his openers about the harsh winter weather, the wife's need to stop on the road a little earlier than he'd planned. But it isn't necessary. The man in the yellow undershirt and the shapeless brown fedora knows the drill. He is well aware that people walking into the office of his motel generally do so in order to rent a room for the night. They aren't just stopping by to say hello.

The proprietor pulls himself away from the seemingly benign yet ever calculating gaze of Bierelane Leonard and looks my father up and down. "Name on top," he says, sliding a white 3 X 5 notecard and a golf pencil across the glass counter-top. "License plate underneath."

The man then proceeds to give my father the brief, iron-bending eye contact he saves for all the underage clientele from the college, implying—*No beer, no sex, no radio playing*—and turns again to Bierelane Leonard, who as far as anyone knows is still out there. Armed and dangerous.

The motelkeeper, who is sure all true villains are smilers, memorizes Leonard's face and, as a habitual reflex, feels for the .22 he has stored under the counter next to the cash box. He has no doubt whatsoever that darkness can take the form of people. He served his term in Korea, and he knows it for a fact.

As for my father, he is stunned at the ease of this business. (The man is barely looking at him!) He takes up the pencil and writes first the license number of the VW (AQB 593) and then the names:

Mr. and Mrs. Aaron Shevach of Cottage Grove

He writes these names on the notecard automatically, without thinking, then crosses them out immediately when he sees what he has done. He didn't quite have a formal plan worked out for the paperwork once he got in here, but Aaron Shevach is the last name on earth he'd wanted to use. Actually, Aaron is his best friend, the only other Jewish kid he knows at the university, who had to move home at the beginning of the year because he had a brain tumor. And now my father has written his name down on the card. Aaron, who right at this moment is dying at the home of his parents on Silver Acre Road, who sent him a letter recently that was written on an envelope folded inside another envelope. "Miss you, Charley" is what he thinks the letter was trying to say. "Dun't have a thought in my goddamn skull."

My father swallows and blinks. The pencil in his fingers is slippery. "Do you think I could get another one?" he asks, motioning toward the stack of fresh notecards, and the guy says: "Sure, Aaron. Whatever you want."

Meanwhile, back in the Karmann Ghia, the Shirelles have long finished singing to my mother, and the heater is faltering. She has the chills, and the windows are all fogged up now, too. It's precipitating. I wasn't there, but I'm certain water had to fall. Everything both tiny and momentous in an Oregon childhood happens in the rain. I'd love, for purposes of surprise, to tell you it wasn't, that the sky was black as an empty well and the wind was scattering stars. But in actuality, there is cloud cover, not a constellation in sight, and she is still waiting with her purse in her lap, holding the strap in one hand, covering the tracheotomy scar on her neck with the other. She almost died. The doctors said she was lucky they were able to reach the growth on her vocal cords at all, and that the marks on her neck will not be red for much longer. The scar will "pink," the doctors say, and if it doesn't pink in six months, well . . . they can do a skin graft.

My father stuffs the problem notecard into the pocket of his raincoat and realizes, unfortunately, that since the man has already called him Aaron, he has no other choice but to repeat the same mistake. He writes "Mr. and Mrs. A. Shevach" on the second card all over again and since his hands are shaking now, he even adds insult to injury by repeating the name slowly out loud, just to make sure it's sunk in.

"It's Aaron and Shirley Shevach," he hears himself say, wincing at the way Shirley and Shevach sound together. He can't imagine where he got that name Shirley anyway. By now it's painfully obvious to my father that this man not only sees the terror in him but smells it, too, like musk off a trapped skunk. In fact, my father realizes, he may as well have walked into this office with a megaphone in his hand.

"Hey, Captain Johnson," he should have screamed into the bullhorn. "You see that virgin out there in the car? Yeah, the one in the idling VW, buddy. The tap-dancing girl with the black hair and the red lips and that weird sexy scar. Yeah. She may not look like anything to you, Fedora, but the one out there in the pretty spearmint outfit with the pearl necklace and the matching little shoes—I'm going to fuck her there in one of your cheap and shitty little rooms. I'm going to change the course of our whole lives in this establishment. Now— tonight—right this minute. What do you think?"

My father covers the second card with both hands. "Sorry," he says. "I keep on making mistakes."

"That's okay, kid," says the Fedora. "Room 17."

It takes only a minute to retrieve the ice bucket, the key with the little anchor on it, two fresh towels. But my father is still pushing the envelope. "The wife," he says, jabbing a hitch-hiker's thumb toward the parking lot. "The missus. We really appreciate the service, right off the freeway like this. The sign was funny, too, that seagull. Very convenient."

The Fedora nods and crosses his arms. "My rooms are six dollars, fifty. I take cash."

"Sounds good," my father says, peeling out the bills with about 95 percent more enthusiasm than is necessary.

He's got eight dollars altogether, singles only, and they're limp as wet leaves after riding the seventeen blocks from the dorm in his back pocket. They're also bunched in there with the one condom he's been carrying around since his graduation from Fort Vancouver Ari Shalom last May, and it all comes out together—some scraps of currency, then this prophylactic device in silver foil.

"Okay, then," my father says, sliding the wad of money toward the man as he shoves the object in question back into the pocket of his raincoat. "That should be about right."

"Looks like you've got change coming," the motelkeeper says, but by the time he looks up from the cash box, my father and his condom have already disappeared.

Several seconds later, through the round peephole she has smudged for herself on the foggy windshield, my mother watches my father rush out of the motel office. He charges around to her side of the car in what looks like a terrible hurry, and raps on the window.

"What took you so long?" she says, rolling it down a crack. "I'm freezing."

Given the recent situation with the notecards and the you-know-what, my father has no idea how to respond, but he makes the best of it. He gives my mother the towels and the keys to Room 17 and tells her to hustle in there. Immediately. He will meet her in a minute, he explains, because he's got things to do. He's just getting ice is all. He's parking the car, getting them settled, i.e., Handling the Administrative End.

"Who needs ice?" my mother hears herself say, then instantly regrets it. Her sorority sister Cassie Campbell would have gone to the room without protest. The wild girl, the fun girl, the hellcat. Cassie would go directly to the room when she was asked and get straight into her baby-doll pajamas. My mother tries her best to smile at him. "Ice is fine," she says. "Whatever you want."

Once she is gone and my father is left alone, he becomes aware of something strange. The harder and faster he moves across the wet parking lot, the more the ice machine seems to retreat. It starts to feel, in fact, like he and the ice machine are playing tag with each other and he is IT. As if that weren't enough, the rain has decided to really pelt him, too, as if the sky is throwing pins.

By the time he arrives at his destination and finds nothing inside the ice machine except the cold metal scoop, my father is exhausted. Why does everyone he loves (including the president) have to die?

Meanwhile, back at the ranch. My mother hangs the towels my father has given her in the tiny motel bathroom, then stands in the middle of Room 17 wondering what to do next. For the time being, she has placed herself in the center of the space, which encircles her like a furniture showroom. Table, mirror, Bible, painted-over rear window. Bed.

The mirror is full-length, framed on the backside of the bathroom door, and it glowers at her from the corner of its eye. This expression of distaste on the mirror's part is unnecessary, however. My mother knows without a piece of glass having to tell her that she is not as beautiful as Cassie Campbell. She is well aware, thank you very much, that Cassie Campbell broke up with Stan Frewing (who was prelaw) to date my father (who was undeclared) for seven weeks. She knows they were seen all over campus, carrying on late into the night. This is what the Pi Phis said, the Kappa Kappa Gammas, the Delta Thetas. The entire female half of the Greek system has been apprised of the fact that they went to the Cheerful Tortoise across from the Capitol to hear improvisational jazz almost every night and that they told the bartender, whom Cassie is quote, "close with," that they were Mr. and Mrs. Charles Campbell and that they were served gin lemon after gin lemon and that they danced until all hours with artists and heroin addicts and bohemians, gaining very valuable life experience that she, Mary Jane, can never compete with, given the fact that the only place of interest she has ever been to is a bomb shelter in St. Helen's with her parents and her pajamas on under her regular clothes.

Wishing she had the courage to shatter herself into a thousand bleeding pieces, my mother turns from the mirror and moves to the nightstand. She picks up the Gideon Bible, places it with great care on the top shelf of the small closet, apologizes to God, then returns to the center of the room, forcing her mind to involve itself with a painting nailed over the bed depicting a busy canal scene somewhere in Venice, Italy. She sees gondoliers, fruit sellers, dense amber sunshine. If someone asked her whether or not she liked the painting, she would tell them she didn't, but somehow, even though the figures in the scene look hurriedly sketched and blurry, hardly like people at all, she is sure they are quite satisfied. They inhabit the lively marketplace of a mediocre painting, and she is sure they are fine with it. They sing. They paddle. They speak fluent Italian. Why can't she be happy? Why can't she speak one of the romance languages?

Approximately five minutes later, my father enters Room 17 with his empty ice bucket to find my mother sitting on the edge of the bed wearing nothing but a bra and what looks to be a full-length slip. She's got her arms crossed over her chest so he can't see the bra itself, but he knows it's under there, and he is unprepared, frankly, for a gesture this powerful or direct.

"Surprise," my mother says, unconsciously reaching up to cover her scar. She sits up a little straighter, waiting for my father to ply her with compliments. To rush across the room and toss himself into her arms. But the boy in the doorway falters. He adjusts his glasses and looks away from the girl on the bed.

Now, I swear he didn't do it on purpose. There was a lot of terror involved, a lot of respect. Nothing in his brief life had prepared him for a sight like this, and even if it had, I'm afraid, it was already too late.

My mother has seen him flinch at the sight of her. She has seen him set down what he is carrying and not know what to do with his hands. I wasn't there, but I can imagine her sitting stiffly, in the thin white slip, watching my father fiddle with some coins in the pocket of his raincoat, and I'd like to convince her, even though I couldn't if I tried, that he isn't thinking about Cassie Campbell right now, because truly, he isn't. He and Cassie, they never really had anything to talk about, what with my father's obvious inexperience regarding all things female and Cassie's tendency to spend their evenings together crying on his shoulder about her vague suspicions regarding Stan Frewing's "secret sexuality."

Unfortunately, despite everyone's best efforts, a paralyzing black silence descends on Room 17. All you can hear is the bathroom faucet dripping a little, the buzz from the old fluorescent bulb.

"Want to know what I did while you were gone?" my mother blurts at last, unable to stop herself from trying to save the day. "I said the Lord's Prayer. Maybe even some Psalms." She watches my father take his hands out of his pockets and wipe them down the ironed crease of his chinos. "Don't you think that was ridiculous? Wasn't it just dumb?"

Still unable to look at her, my father manages to shake his head. "I think that's good," he says. "Prayers are good."

"You don't think that. Not really."

"I do."

My father feels the weight of the car keys in his pocket. He hears the faint sigh of the freeway, the distant call of a train. If he had the nerve, he'd cut it with the shy nonsense and march right over there. He'd do whatever it is grown men are rumored to do with scantily clad women in cheap rented rooms. But all he seems able to think of at the moment is the man in the fedora, Captain Johnson, who, given the problem with the birth-control item from earlier, might definitely be on to them. He'll probably (if he hasn't already) even call the state police, don't you think? And before the night is over, there'll be a very serious APB out on the license plate of that VW. Not even his VW actually, but the VW he inherited recently from his best friend, Aaron Shevach, who is dying right this minute, cut down in the prime of his youth by a brain tumor, and he, Chuck, *Charley*, who doesn't have a thought left in his skull, has stupidly, *stupidly*, placed their names on the register as Mr. and Mrs. Aaron Shevach. So the APB will match.

"Shit," my father bursts out, then covers his mouth. "God-dammit—fuck."

My mother watches wide-eyed as my father tenses up like some kind of lunatic. He's shifting his weight all over the place, can't find a comfortable way to stand.

"I guess I'm just going over things in my head from earlier" is all he can think to tell her when she asks what's going on. "You know, with the guy. In the motel office."

"What about him?"

"He was just weird, is all."

"You mean crazy?"

"I don't know."

My father cracks open a peephole in the venetian blinds and scans the parking lot. "I think I'll cover the license plates on the car or something," he says, then glances over his shoulder at her as if she isn't half naked, as if she and her underthings are just occurrences of the common everyday. "It won't take long" is what he says. "Just stand up for a second, okay?"

Silently and without looking at him (not once!), my mother peels up the chenille bedspread and drapes herself with it. Against every fluid ounce of her better judgment, she rises, much like the president's widow in a long gown, and does as she is asked, standing near the nightstand, with great dignity, in her opinion, while the individual who seemingly has brought her to Captain Johnson's Oceanside only to reject her throws the pillows to the carpet and hurriedly strips the blanket from the bed.

"I'll be right back. I promise," she hears this person say as he hightails his bundle toward the door of Room 17. "All right?"

My mother doesn't answer. If she is left in this room, she decides, he will return to find it empty. The bedspread tightens around her shoulders and her jaw sets. You'll be sorry, she vows to him as his hand inches toward the doorknob. You absolutely will.

Oblivious to the silent oath that has just been cast, my father pulls out the car keys and cracks the portal that represents every decision he will make for the rest of his life. He looks back at my mother wrapped in bed linens and has no idea that he'll marry her, that they'll have three children together, that they'll become millionaires and lose it all just as quickly, that they'll betray each other with several of their friends.

"See you in a second," he says, pausing at the threshold. "Okay?"

My mother doesn't answer. Instead she lifts her right hand and, with a surgeon's precision, begins to follow the scythelike curl of the scar from the base of her earlobe to her collarbone. Up and down. Down and up. She really doesn't mean to cry. She wasn't planning on it, but the tears just come. Hot and angry at first. Then quieter, empty.

Only inches away from an entirely different life, my father freezes in the doorway and listens to my mother's breath catch. Displays of the emotional kind like this will always petrify him, but he knows, must have known, that he is being given an option here with infinite branching possibilities. He could exit right now, for instance, and defray the cost of the lace wedding invitations, the off-white mother-to-be dress from Lipman Wolfe, the chiffon cake with raspberry/lemon insides that was such a bitch to pick out.

My father clutches the prickly motel-issue blanket against his chest. He doesn't know quite what to do here, and can you blame him? If you could imagine the consequences of your future, would you still walk into it?

Time slows to a trickle for about a hundredth of a second, but I'm relieved to report that my father's indecision doesn't last. In spite of the frog's blood and the crooked hems, in spite of the trying hard and the failing, and the understanding that will always come too late. In spite of all the invisible hands that pull any scared boy toward any parking lot at any given time. In spite of all these things, he turns in the direction fate points him in. For some inexplicable reason that will become more and more elusive with each passing year, my father turns. My father turns to my mother and chooses us.

In a burst of desperate confidence, he strides (actually strides!) across the room and pulls her into the folds of his raincoat. He presses her face against the front of his shirt.

"It'll be all right," he says with so much authority it surprises him. "I know what I'm doing. Do you trust me?"

My mother tries to pull away a little at first, but here is where he kisses her. Here is where he leans in awkwardly and their lips make contact. It is a small gesture in the history of the world, butterflies do not cause tornadoes, civilizations do not rise and fall, but for both of them, for now anyway, it is enough.

"How's that?" my father says when he's finished, and my mother smiles then. It's the first real one she's been able to manage tonight, and I have to say, quite honestly, it lights up the room.

"I'm cold," she whispers, curling against him. "Hurry up out there, okay?"

In the parking lot at last, my father stands in front of the domed hood of the Karmann Ghia. By now it has stopped raining, and the stars that shine down, illumining the city of Salem, do so busily, with an almost officious brightness. It is their job to twinkle, and by God they're going to, moon or no moon. But of course there is one of those, too, a huge white lantern of a thing, so brilliant and close to the earth that the man in the fedora comes out to see it.

It's amazing to him how ordered the world seems under the pressure of the moon's lowering light. How straight the freeway, how strict the rows of Douglas fir lining the horizon to a blue vanishing point. The proprietor of the Captain Johnson puffs at the end of a new cigar and watches the smoke wind away into the darkness. The nights in Oregon can be truly beautiful like this after the rain. They'll pay you back for all that gray. Everything is glistening and steaming clean. And the streets are silent. All except for this creepy kid with the shredded old rubber who is obviously up to no good with one of the motel blankets.

The Fedora stubs out the cigar and begins the long stroll across the tarmac. Now, he put that kid all the way down at the end so he wouldn't have to deal with him anymore tonight. These first-timers who want to have sex in his rooms should just go ahead and have it. He's used fake names before, and he knows how the world works. This is why he owns a motel in the first place.

As the proprietor makes his calculated approach from the left, my father, who has been watching the man lurk outside the motel office, gets a little jumpy. He is excellent at physics, but he still cannot get the blanket to stay. He has tried stuffing it under the windshield wipers, tucking it into the cracks at the side of the hood.

"Looks like you got a problem there, son," the Fedora says. "You want to tell me about it?"

My father swallows what feels like a dry athletic sock. "It's just the battery on this thing," he explains. "I'm trying to keep it warm, you know? It loses too much heat"—he takes a pause as the man crosses his arms, waiting—"through the hood."

No words are necessary. This is the most ridiculous thing the motelkeeper has probably ever heard in his life, and they both know it.

"Well, good," my father says, handing the man the wet blanket. "That's probably safe enough for now."

"Mm-hmm."

And then they eye each other. The man who's been to war and the boy who's about to go. It's just a glance, a quickie, but the contact holds.

You take it easy, kid, the Fedora wants to say. There's no reason to get so wound up. Fear is a killer. Just ask Bierelane Leonard. But the man doesn't say anything, and in the end he doesn't have to. He watches my father walk away into his life. He sees the door of Room 17 open in a burst of yellow light, then witnesses that light swallow the boy up. And this is where the story ends. I'd love to tell you everything that happens next, but I'm afraid the narrator must pull away now and allow the fates to step in. An egg demands a sperm here. Inevitability demands its privacy.

What I can promise, however, is that tonight, despite all the odds, my parents share the bed together very well. Destiny has given them a cameo, and they bathe in its fragile limelight. Cassie Campbell is not on either of their minds, or the Fedora. Not even Priscilla or Aaron Shevach. When sleep comes, it is tangled and soft and deep.

In God's point of view, He loves them. He wants to gather them and roll them into a ball, like wool. He, for one, appreciated my mother's apology, and He'll give them a story together for better or worse. All aboard the same small ship with Captain Johnson at the helm.

And overhead, high above the cloudless city, the statue of the Golden Pioneer keeps watch from the dome of the State Capitol Building less than a mile away.

He is standing thirty feet tall behind his plow, gazing down at the still-innocent sleepers, whispering to them in their dreams: To all souls resting here amid these sovereign lands, I bless thee. I beg thee reap thy harvest in glory. I bid thee peace.

FUCK YOU

He was in a baseball uniform. Age twelve or thirteen, maybe, but it was hard to tell. Boys mature so much slower than girls.

I was in the Buick with a trunkful of groceries. It was Saturday. Jack was at work. The air-conditioning was broken, so all the windows were down to let in the breeze. Plywood and cement dust. New fertilizer.

He was sitting on a bag of bark dust at the four-way stop. Gray uniform, lots of stains. The baseball hat, it might have been on backward or hanging off the knee. I'll always remember that it was red.

I nosed the car up to the white line. As usual, nobody else was around. No gardeners in the yards, or even dogs. But there he was. The first thing with a heartbeat I'd seen.

Food spoils fast in the heat, but I could already feel myself leaning forward, reaching as far across the seat as my stomach would let me.

"Everything okay, here?" I called out the window. "You lost?"

He glanced over briefly, then shrugged me off like he couldn't be bothered. It was understandable, really. If I was him, I wouldn't have paid much attention either.

I adjusted my sticky dress. Pushed the hair out of my face. "Not in the mood for talking, huh?" I said. "Same here. Hate it actually."

No reply on that one as well. Not a word, but the woman who was playing me felt herself smiling. She looked at my hand, the palm that belonged to me, sliding across the seat and patting the leather.

"Buses don't stop here yet," I heard myself explain. "Why don't you hop in and I'll run you home?"

I reached under the seat for the cigarette stash. By the time I found one and got it going, he was blinking in at me sideways. Eyes like glossed wood, a splatter of tough-looking freckles.

"I don't know you," he said.

I nodded in complete agreement. "Technically, that's true," I said. "But I probably know your mother."

His eyes stayed on me, flickering. "Where from?"

I squinted past him a little, at the thirsty line of shrubs they were planting on the median. "From school."

"I've never seen you there."

"Maybe you weren't looking."

I tossed my purse in the backseat and gunned the engine. Once, twice. "And I'm not your driver, either," I said, pressing both pedals down hard. "Walk home if you want to, I don't care."

I released my foot from the brake, edging forward by inches, and it worked like magic.

He tossed the mitt in first, then opened up the door. If he noticed my condition, it didn't register on his face. Be fruitful and multiply, I felt like saying, but I didn't. Sometimes phrases just pop into my head.

The mitt was filthy and swollen. It rested on the seat

between us like a rotting hand. The leather had a smell, and the smell had a taste. Like childhood, maybe. Like birth.

"A catcher?"

"Mm-hmm."

"Where's your mask?"

"Coach keeps it," he said. "Masks are worth a lot of money."

I nodded, but he was hardly looking at me. As far as we were both concerned, I could've been a ghost.

Across the intersection, I noticed some stray workers straddling the skeletons of new houses. One man standing on the platform of an upstairs braced his shoulders, and the circular saw screamed as he slid it through the wood.

"Win or lose today?" I asked, shifting the idle into park.

"Only practice."

"You practice in the uniform?"

"Coach says we have to."

"Well." My finger traced the outside of the steering wheel. "Coaches are stupid. Adolf Hitler was a coach."

"He was?"

I went for the cigarettes a second time, and he watched me, blinking patiently through grimy bangs. Waiting, like children do, I suppose, for the adults to shut the fuck up.

"Where to?" I asked, expecting something just around the corner. It was a surprise when he mumbled an address at the far end of the viaduct. "What are you doing all the way up here?"

He ignored the question and spit out his gum, going for my ashtray. I reached across, and his wrist stopped in my hand. I only held on for a second, but I could feel it through the skin. His ordinariness.

"Cigarettes only," I told him. "You'll have to put it some-where else."

"Where?"

I held out my hand. "Here."

His head jerked in my direction like a surprised little chip-munk. "Go ahead," I told him. "Let go. It won't hurt any-thing."

I cupped my free hand, wiggled the fingers a bit, and the gum plopped into my palm. Gray and mottled as a little brain.

"See?" I said, sticking my arm out the window and bringing it back in again. "All gone."

"That's littering."

"It's okay. It's not even a neighborhood yet. Nobody cares."

He slouched a little lower in the seat, trying to hide a smile.

"What's your name?"

"Sev."

"Is that a nickname or real?"

He tapped his finger against the automatic lock button. "Real," he said, but I doubted it.

I glanced into the rearview mirror, and my own two eyes stared back. "Well, listen, Sev," I said. "There's ice cream in the trunk. Maybe you wouldn't mind if we stop home first, put it away?"

From the driveway he watched me take Jack's key from under the brick, then haul the groceries out of the trunk to the kitchen door. He didn't offer to help when he came up the porch, and I didn't ask.

"This'll just take a minute," I told him. "Look around."

Still shy, he tapped his cleats against the doorjamb, leaving little clots of mud I knew would dry into a silty dust. I saw him look at the scattered boxes when he came inside, but he didn't mention them. Just stepped over the balled-up newspaper and kept on going.

I left him to wander and stuffed the food in the cupboards. Taco shells and fancy bean dip. Jack's steaks.

By the time I'd finished and stuck my head out the window,

his legs were in the pool. The cleats, tied by the shoe strings, hung around his neck. For a long time he didn't see me, staring.

"Hey," I called out finally, and he started. Pulled his legs out of the water.

"Don't worry about it," I said. "Nobody minds. You want anything to drink? I don't know what kids like. Kool-Aid? Hawaiian Punch?"

He made a horrible face, and I made one right back. "Don't worry," I said. "I don't have them anyway."

I noticed his eyes widen when I waddled out the sliding door and set the last bottle of Jack's Heineken down next to him. "I know," I said, before he could argue. "But it's okay. We can share. I'm not allowed to drink it either."

"Hmm." He dipped his fingers in the water and made designs on the surface. There were fine spider hairs on his arms that glowed in the sun, little scrapes on the back of his hands.

I knew I was supposed to take him right home, do the responsible thing, but the company relaxed me. I reached down, took a quick sip of the beer I'd given him, and the taste almost made me faint.

"So," I said, lowering myself into a chaise a few feet away. "What do you think of the place?"

"It's nice."

I lit another cigarette. "It's new."

"Do you live here by yourself?"

"I live here with Jack."

"Oh."

Up above us, small planes were making white crisscrosses in the sky. Only lines, not really spelling anything. I closed my eyes and started to hum a little. Just some snippets of things. No melody. When I heard his voice again, it almost made me jump.

"How come you don't unpack?" He had blurted it out but kept his eyes on the water. There were some leaves floating in it. Bugs.

I held my smoke in for a long time, watching him bang his heels against the side of the pool.

"Care if I sit next to you?" I said, hefting myself up out of the chair.

He turned and squinted back at me. "It's your pool."

"Right," I said. "Scoot over."

I cupped my free arm under my stomach and sank onto the tile beside him. The water sucked up my legs, cool as blue gelatin. Maybe I could see now why Jack had said he wanted one.

I leaned back, and we were quiet for a long time. Not embarrassed. Just looking at the water together. Looking at the sky. There were yellow jackets flying over the pool, and we watched them, too. Skimming the surface, trying not to drown.

"You have a pool, Sev?"

He looked up at me as if the answer were obvious. "Nah."

"This pool was the first thing they built here," I said. "Before they even built the stupid house."

"Really?"

"Really. That's just how they do it, builders. Because they're goddamn idiots."

I saw the word travel up his spine. A current of electricity. He sat up straighter, listening.

I scooted a little closer. "You want to know something?" I whispered. "I don't unpack because I just don't. You know when you're supposed to do something and all you can think about is not doing it? Like cleaning up after somebody and taking out the trash. I bet you hate that. Do you hate it?"

"Sure." He nodded. "But I hate other things more."

In the water, our four feet were kicking in rhythm like a strange animal running. I could feel his sleeve when he moved, brushing lightly against my arm.

"Like what?" I said. "What do you hate?"

He looked at me like I was dim. "You know," he said, tossing the answer out as if it were spit. "Las Palmas."

"What's Las Palmas?"

"My school," he said, rolling his eyes. "I thought you said you knew."

I took another swig of the beer before he could say anything else. Yeasty and bitter. "I do," I said, "but school's a boring thing to hate. Try something else."

"Like what?"

I dunked my hands in the water and swished them around. "Like people telling you you'll be a great mother and they don't even know you. Like your husband's friends thinking you don't notice them staring at your gorilla tits whenever you cross the goddamn room."

I poked him on the leg, and the words came out in a gush. "I bet you hate baseball," I said. "You go to the baseball diamond, whatever it is, and the coach yells at you. You have to roll in the dirt on your face. The pitcher could hit you in the mouth with the ball and make you ugly, give you brain damage. When I was your age, I got hit in the face with a bat."

We both seemed a little shocked. I had never even held a bat.

"Baseball's not like that, really," he said. "But I do hate Bruce."

He looked up at me, waiting for my reaction. The 43 on his chest rose and fell with his breathing. I smiled. "Bruce is an excellent person to hate," I said, tossing my cigarette into the pool. "Who's he?"

"I don't know," he said. "Some guy from FedEx. My mom brought him home in the uniform, and now he thinks he lives with us. He has a puppy that eats its own crap."

I made it a point not to react. "People do that, too," I said, elbowing his shoulder.

"They do not," he said. *"Liar."*

Once he said it, I felt better, lighter somehow. I pulled my leg back and kicked water all the way across the pool. It glittered in the air like broken glass. I put my hand out, inviting him to give it a try, but he had stopped kicking. "Seriously," he said. "She could marry him."

I nodded. "Probably. But then they'll get divorced, so it won't be so bad. Bad things never last." I picked up some water and flicked it at him. "What's the worst thing you can say?" I said. "Ever. Ever-ever-ever. Say it."

He looked a little scared. "I don't know," he said. "Why?"

"Oh, come on," I said. "I'm just a fat lady from the circus. Nobody cares."

He ran his hands along his shins. They looked elongated under the water. "I don't know," he said again. "I'm not allowed to say the F-word."

"I'm not, either," I said smiling. "But fuck that."

I kicked some water toward him, and he kicked it back. "Come on," I said. "Don't be a baby. Say 'Bruce is a mother-fucker.' Say it."

Water caught in his eyelashes, and he wiped it away, grinning at me with a mouth full of dirty teeth.

"I do hate the coach, actually," he said. "He pulled me out of the game today, and we lost."

I stopped kicking. "Thought it was only practice. *Liar.*"

"Well." He smiled and looked down, then kicked a huge wave. "Fuck losing."

"Yeah," I said. "And fuck your mother for screwing a mail-man. Fuck the birds and bees too, while you're at it. Fuck Jack."

A wave from our kicking swelled over the side of the pool and soaked the hem of my dress. I grabbed a fistful of water and threw it at the house. "Splash harder," I said. "Do it!"

I kicked water as high as I could, and it pelted down around us like hail. "Fuck all the people in this desert," I said. "Fuck humanity, period! Fuck this house!"

I was on a roll then, and I admit it, I picked up an armful of water and tossed it in his lap, soaking the uniform.

"Oops," I said, snorting, and he looked at me then with a hard boy's face. The kind of boy who throws cats off high bridges and laughs while they fall. His face was a smear when he finally said it:

"Fuck you."

He stopped his kicking and moved away a little, waiting for me to react. Waves broke over the sides of the pool like a storm.

There was a movement near the fence. Maybe just a bird, but I thought I saw a flash of someone's knit shirt on the other side. It was possible, or maybe I had just imagined it. Anyway, I didn't care. I clapped my hand down on his knee. It wasn't sexual, and it wasn't pathetic. It was just a skinny kid's leg in nylon baseball pants.

"Thanks, Sev," I said, giving the bone a squeeze before taking away my hand. "Fuck you, too, kid. Fuck both of us, right?"

"Right." He smiled at me shyly, then lay back on the concrete, staring up.

In my stomach I could feel my own son doing the same thing through closed eyelids. Just floating there. Recording everything.

"You can swim here anytime you want to, you know," I said after a while. "Come after practice sometime if you feel like it. I don't mind taking you home."

He nodded but kept looking up, past me. Eyes dilated with sky. The water easing up our legs gently now, then back down.

When I was his age, I thought adults were like gods. Lightning came from their fingers, and their words were like thunder and fire.

I lowered myself back onto my elbows and looked up where he was looking. In the distance somewhere a dog was barking. Over and over without any purpose. The kind of barking where you know all it wants is to hear the sound of its own voice.

MY NAME

The files say Verta's wacked. But she can't help it. She's old. She can't remember what war it was her kid died in, even if I do. And he bit it. Jesus, did he. I won't remind her, because I can tell she's thinking about him already, the way she's staring. Verta's looking at nothing every five minutes. At what's left of her kid, most likely, his memory splattered all over those green drapes.

"It was the jungle, Verta," I say, lifting her from that chair she's peed in, carrying her like the wet mother of Jesus over to that bed. *"The jungle."*

But when I lay her down to change her diapers on the shiny plastic coverlet, little, bony Verta reaches up out of nowhere and grabs the collar of my whites like a skeleton hauling itself back up from the grave.

"Buck," she says, speaking a word now for the first time in the twelve days we have been acquainted. Her voice smaller than a newborn kitten's. "Buck."

This name hovering there between us like an eyelash flutter, a butterfly kiss.

"Well, sure," I tell Verta, once my heart has stopped its breathless racing. "That's right, exactly."

It's just that Verta's a vegetable who never talks. And Buck is not my name.

After I was done at Rawlins Correctional USMC, everybody there got friendly all of a sudden and asked me questions.

"Hey, Van Hoomison," they said. "How about cleaning up some oldies for money down at Salem State? How about some housing on the grounds in trade for light janitorial? A white uniform? Your own shower and towels?"

"Sounding good," I said to them. "Sounding like a winner."

So a floor full of yowling oldies is what I got. I got Ben-Goopy-Barber, for instance, in Number 9 North, with his crushed bananas and his rocking chair. But then I got my prize, too. My Verta ten doors down. Making up for everything with that trembling almost-whimper, those ghostly eyes. "Aqua-Verta Eyes," I call them, and I could almost write a song about it if I had any music in me. About human eyes with nothing in them. Eyes like flat blue water you could fill up with any reflection you might like to. And when I told the probation people at Rawlins about Verta's eyes, about the waxy blue emptiness, about that hero of a son she had who came apart at the seams in a firefight that happened once in the part of Phu Vang where the sand cliffs look down on the sea, right away they were all smiles.

"A little compassion inside the old Van Hoomison, eh?" they said, and the big shrink in charge gave me an elbow to the ribs.

Next free chance I got after morning clean-up, I read for "compassion" in *Merriam-Webster's Collegiate Dictionary.* In the copy I found inside Pretty Nurse Nobody's Plexiglas capsule, down below on the shelf behind her phone books and her French-language flash cards and the to-go forks and knives she keeps from the cafeteria where both of us take our meals on separate sides. The *M.W.C.D.* And in there, after the cover page where somebody wrote, *To Jonna Lee, Love Peter. Class of '67 Rules*, I saw on page 191, they had it written down as a pity.

"A pity," it said, "that inclines one to help."

Under that they had "compatible," and under that "compatriot," which was my favorite. "A fellow countryman," it said. "Able to co-exist." "Compeer" was next, which I hadn't ever heard of before, or cared to, and then "compel," which I was just getting into when Pretty Nurse Nobody tapped on my shoulder with her frost-tipped fingernail.

"Excuse me," she said, her eyes dropping to my name label. "Mr. Van Hoomison." And then she took that dictionary away.

"I was a fellow countryman, you see," I explain to Verta after lunch, my bath mittens rubbing brisk circles from her toes and on up. "A fellow countryman of Buck. Your son.

"Of Buckman Scrivner," I say extra loud, hoping she'll be reminded of the morning. Of what she tried to call me. And I try and direct her eyes to the picture I put in a frame of my buddy Pink Hensleigh in his full-dress blues, who watches over her for me from the nightstand all the days and nights. Hensleigh, shy and mild, half-smiling at the camera with a closed mouth to cover his gold front tooth.

"Almost like your kid, right?" I say, pointing over at Hensleigh. "Brave, too." But Verta's eyes show no recognition, no resistance to the soapy bath mittens I'm wearing when they return to her pale blue shins, polishing them with care like the finest antique automobile.

"Buck," I whisper to Verta. Leaning now over her lovely, ruined face. "Be a good girl. Say it again."

And as I cradle her in the terry towel, my fingers combing through the thin puff of white hair on her freckly scalp, Pink Hensleigh is watching over us from his pulpit on the nightstand. "You see it now finally, don't you, Van Hoomie?" he says. "The Mercy. Am I right?"

At Rawlins Correctional, I was not uncomfortable. I had eighteen months' worth of rivets to file down. I had women like I always do. In magazines. Then, all at once, I was downstairs at the window slot with my cardboard box, my papers, dog-tags, my fatigues.

"Okay, Van Hoomison," they said, opening up the outside door. "There you are, buddy. There you go."

Down the basement of 9 North are the secret files of every person in Salem State. It's where the doctors go to find things, the nurses. Pretty Nurse Nobody, who is not a boss but close, made it clear I am never allowed down there, but in my opinion, what I can find everywhere else is mine to touch. Files on counters, on silver wheeled trays. Files that hang on beds and stick up out of open drawers. And I search until I find it in a pile outside F Lab: the sand cliffs, the silver-starred son of hers, the South China Sea. Verta Jane Scrivner's medical life there for me in the colors of a thousand pens. Pages all titled with the same:

Resultive Catalepsy / Catatonia
Catastrophic Loss.

Next time I see her alone, Pretty Nurse Nobody is inside her plastic capsule with the imperial watering can, giving drinks to her succulents.

"If a person's got catalepsy," I ask through the airhole, "what happens with that?"

"Well, nothing, Mr. Van Hoomison," she says. "Catalepsy is bad."

"Bad?"

"Yes, Mr. Van Hoomison. Very bad. One cannot talk, and one's muscles go rigid."

"But what if there is talking? What if there's a word?"

"It doesn't mean anything. Things are generally *sans espoir*."

"What's *sans espoir*?"

"Hope, Mr. Van Hoomison. As in there is none of it. Now may I ask you to please step back?"

Once I've dried and powdered the rest of my afternoon oldies, I put a velvet bow-clip in Verta's hair in honor of her speaking and take a special picture of her with the Polaroid I found in the doctors' coatroom. An SX-70 Land camera and two cartridges of color film.

The files say with movements and sounds sometimes there's a little delay, so when the flash pops silver, it's a long minute before Verta's eyes squeeze shut, then flutter wide.

"Verta. Cheese," I say, and then I scoot her over a bit to make some room for myself next to her on the bed so we can watch her develop out of the green chemicals.

"Here," I say, bending her fingers around the white border one at a time like soft modeling clay. "This is you."

And I make sure to point out to Verta how, in the picture, her left eye seems to be closing by accident and looks like she might be meaning to wink. This picture of her I set on the nightstand next to Hensleigh's, and I can't help looking at the two of them for a while. Pink's stiffened smile. Verta's claw-fingers curled in the air above her chest as if the photo is still held in them. Then I try and go.

"See you tomorrow," I tell the room. I stand in the doorway then, for a minute, turn off and on the light. But every time I flip the switch up, Verta's still lying there on her back with her mouth open, keeping track of the shadows on the ceiling.

"Buck," I imagine her saying. "Buck, please don't go."

So I take a quick stroll down to Ben Barber's room for a whiff of some predictable air. Open and close his door a couple times. Flip on and off his lights. And when I feel a little calmer,

I hustle down to the chapel in the sub-basement and start to buff the floors like I'm supposed to, but there's barely enough time to get the cord untangled before I'm back upstairs again. Avoiding her door and the puffy-tissue decorations they smothered it with for the bicentennial. Checking in on every other bedridden oldie I can find, even the ones I hate, until finally, the whispery squish of my white loafers on the floor is something I can't stand to hear another minute, and the whole flow of the hallway routine in 9 North starts to really give me the peeves all of a sudden. The way Pretty Nurse Nobody will slice me with her eyes as she wheels the oldies by me to the activity room. The way she darts their chairs around my knees in quick little arcs at the last minute, as if I am some kind of roadblock. And the other oldies that are just on their own to wander, they are bothering me, too, especially the ones who are barefooted, tiny-stepping along with their rolling IVs on a leash.

"Stop staring," I want to tell them, even though they don't even see or sense me and have no idea of the world left at all, much less the true story of why I am standing here in the first place. About Rawlins Correctional, for starters, and the old lady behind the cash register at the Deli Mart in Forest Grove. The stupid old lady in the terry-cloth sweatsuit, who got so scared of me that day in my full-dress blues, of all the names I was calling out to people who weren't there, that she handed over all the money from the till and her own purse, too. Even though it was a phony gun.

"Okay, Van Hoomison," said Rawlins Bluff Correctional when I saluted them at the door. "There you are, buddy. There you go."

Back in Room 19, I'm sweating now and Verta hasn't moved a millimeter, so I give her neck a rub, splash some cold water on my face from her sink. And I am about to march back to the church and follow the rules they have given me. I am about to finish the daily janitorial, like I always do, when it occurs to me: The fire stairs to the sub-basement are only three doors down.

"I have a special trip for you, Verta," I promise her as I slip a second nightie on her so she won't be cold. "How's about a little break?"

For any kind of journey, I'm supposed to roll Verta in a chair, sign her out in the logbook under Number 19, but Verta is lighter in my arms than angel food, and it's just easier during the shift change to carry her out in a blanket, braced tight against my chest.

"I'm fine," I tell her on our way down the stairs. "You're fine, too. Everything is."

Inside, the chapel feels clean, even though the buffer is still out in the middle of the aisle where I left it, and some of the Bibles are scattered around where the other oldies left them after morning service.

"Surprise," I say, but when the swinging doors suck shut behind us, when she feels the chapel's cool, dark hush, instead of perking up, Verta only seems to get worse.

"It's all right," I say, gently bending her at the waist so she fits safely in the second pew. "We're all under control now, right? A-OK."

But as I tuck the blanket over her knees, as I turn to direct her head toward the pink chrysanthemums on the altar, the shiny brass bowl of green chocolate mints, Verta's gone so rigid that I've got to wrap her fingers around the back of the bench in front of her so she doesn't slide on down.

"Gotta go to work now," I tell her. "Finish a couple things." And it isn't until I'm done with the floors and standing up at the podium, scrubbing it down hard with the antiseptic soap, losing myself as I always do, in the battle of making things clean, that I hear her again.

"Buck."

And when I look down at her, at Verta, sitting all alone in the rows of empty pews, staring up, not at me exactly, but close, somewhere past my shoulder, waiting, I can feel the love blood rushing up to my throat, and I have to convince her now, in this church, from this pulpit, why I can never be her boy. Not me. Not Van Hoomison.

"It's *sans espoir*," I tell Verta, bending over the silver microphone. "Hope. As in there is none of it.

"Someplace right next door to Da Nang, for instance," I tell her. "The day the army transport plane got forced to land with a woman inside it. An American captain's wife from Manila and her little girl. Before there was time to secure the area. By accident. The rain a wet brown veil, all the palm trees swinging side to side as if they had hips.

"And if I close my eyes," I tell Verta. "I can remember the green field."

Green field of buffalo grass lashing against our eyes and cheeks.

"Fuck me," said Pink Hensleigh. "Fuck my ass if this is not a miracle."

Because there she was. A woman of the female kind, in a minidress the color of a baby deer. Her patent-leather purse held over her head like a little crown, her daughter pressed against her as they were hustled, both of them, into their own separate tent.

"Like a queen of mercy," Hensleigh said. "Like butter or better."

"Stay away from her," everybody was yelling. "Motherfuckers, stay back."

But there was Hensleigh with me. Shy, mild, hothouse-looking Hensleigh, with a big religion and a gold front tooth. They asked us to stay with her, to guard her door.

And I remember us. Staring in at her around the tent flap. The hot mist swirling off our ponchos. "You see, she might have looked," I tell Verta, "like a shivering, muddy Nurse Nobody." That young. That pretty. Except unlike Nurse Nobody, she didn't seem to mind us at all.

"And we just soaked her in," I tell Verta. Like when you look at a bright color and it almost hurts your eyes.

"You see it, Van Hoomie?" Hensleigh said. "Love everywhere."

And when he handed me his gun, I held it for him. Held it barrel upward and filling with rain as he walked without me right into that tent.

"Ma'am," he said to the queen.

And he knelt there at her feet, right in front of her little girl, with the water brimming off the front of his helmet, dripping down on his hands like big tears.

"Do you know," he said, tapping the gold tooth, "how I got this damn thing?"

And when the little girl and her mother shook their heads no, no, they didn't, Pink Hensleigh laughed. "No reason," he said. "Weird, right? The baby tooth, it just died in there. Big one never grew in over it to fill the space."

"Pink," I told him. "You better get back out here."

But Hensleigh, I tell Verta, he was already making a big show of giving the queen his gold tooth. Showing her the little nub, moving it back and forth so she could see there was still a root.

"I'd appreciate it, ma'am," he said, "if you'd keep this one for me. You and your girl might be the only real ladies from our side to ever visit Da Nang. The only ones."

And when it was time for them to get escorted back to the plane, it was Hensleigh who raised his hand to take them when I refused to volunteer. Hensleigh who carried the little girl in his arms while the queen ran along next to him, his gold tooth in her purse. Hensleigh who put his hand on her waist and lifted her, one-handed, into the beating belly of the helicopter. Even Hensleigh with the best view when the ruffle on the minidress blew up because she lifted both hands from it to wave goodbye. And finally, as the queen rose over us, up and up into the smoke and water and electric blue gas, it was Hensleigh who bought sniper fire on the way back. Jesus, did he. His body dancing with enough bullets that when they stopped, he was still hanging there for just a second, still guarding that green field like a mute, raggedy scarecrow, held up there by strings until it was time to come down.

"You see, Verta?" I tell her. "It was love everywhere. Love everywhere."

And when I am done. When I drop my hands from the podium. Search for my Aqua-Verta in the shadowy pews, she is still out there where I put her, but in trouble now. All askew. Tipped over on the bench in the same position. Her lips stuck in the same shape, trying to form a "B."

So I hurry down there to her. To where Verta is, and I gather her. Scoop her, really, into a safe shape that fits my arms. I hold all that frailty against me like it's royalty. It's in every step I take back up the firestairs to Room 19, where my friend Pink Hensleigh will be waiting.

"Good man, Buck," he'll say when we get there, and I'll thank him.

Even though that never is—never was—never will be my name.

GOOD TO HEAR YOU

On the morning two commercial airliners crash into the Twin Towers of the World Trade Center in New York City, my father oversleeps his alarm in Memphis, Tennessee. Unaware of the national disaster now in progress, and running over an hour late, he turns on the shower in the adjoining bathroom to awaken Laurie, his second wife who is still asleep, then shuffles into the kitchen to turn on the coffee machine and feed the cat. In the kitchen alone, my father lights his first cigarette and watches the cat, a skinny stray he found hiding in the barbecue recently, systematically wolf her food. It looks more like backward vomiting than eating, he thinks, but my father watches the meatballs he has prepared for Littleslip (whom he also calls Lovebird sometimes, or Ki Ki) disappear with feral appreciation. If he could, my father imagines, he would live with thousands of cats—*thousands*, if Laurie weren't allergic, but it is nice enough of her to put up with even this one, he reminds himself. Laurie (and it almost brings tears to his eyes to think of it) is a very generous young person.

Just after nine-thirty, Laurie appears in the kitchen in her business suit, and the two leave their house at 7095 Ivy Leaf Circle. They step over the newspaper lying on the doormat, as is their habit, and get into my father's 1989 Honda two-door coupe. My father is behind the wheel in Bermuda shorts, T-shirt, and Italian dress shoes. Laurie is beside him with her open briefcase in her lap, paging through employee pay records that will become vitally necessary to over one hundred thousand people in the hours ahead.

"I love you," she says to him, her eyes still on the computer forms as they pull out of the driveway, and my father answers her as he does to anyone who tells him they love him: "Good to hear you" or "You're my baby," he says, then reaches for the radio knob. It is a habit of years gone by, when he drove expensive sports cars, and all of them, the Austin Healey and the Ferrari, the Alfa, even the rickety vintage Corvette, had radios. But now, as his hand moves toward the dusty space above the gear shift, he remembers: This is Memphis. This is his Honda from the divorce settlement. He doesn't have a radio. It is broken, and he hasn't replaced it.

I like to imagine that when my father reaches for the radio, this is when he remembers us: The underachieving oldest child in Los Angeles with the decent marriage and the temperamental chip on her shoulder. The workaholic youngest with the great job in the Transamerica Building in San Francisco. The video-poker-addicted son back in Oregon who vanished after his discharge from Desert Storm over a decade before.

"Screw the lost radio," he might say to himself whenever he reaches for it. "Where the hell are those children?"

At ten-thirty sharp, my father pulls the Honda to the outer perimeter of a large multinational paper conglomerate and drops Laurie at the watchman's gate. "Don't worry about it," she tells my father when he offers to drive her in past the security checkpoint. "We'll just get a new clock, right?"

"Right," my father says, then watches his second wife disappear through a series of chain-link fences into the executive compound. My father, now a sculptor in bronze and glass who left his obstetrics practice ten years before to become an artist in his mid-fifties and who now takes watercolor classes at Memphis State under the tutelage of a female professor he calls "inarguably brilliant and with an excellent figure," cranks the engine of his Honda. He exits the curving hills of the business park, and drives back home to retrieve his brushes and paints.

An hour later, he sets up an easel on the lawn of a second business park located near the airport on the opposite side of the city. The assignment the professor has given his watercolor class is "Half-Urban Reality," and he has chosen this area because there are two mirrored skyscrapers, one large in the foreground, and one smaller that appears to be reflected inside it, built several miles away. Behind him are the Mississippi River and, extending east and west, rolling hills of puffy green trees.

Before he begins, my father puts on his lucky straw hat and runs a comb through his beard. He slips on the old flowered shirt he bought when he lived on Oahu, changes into his huarache sandals, and adjusts the Bermuda shorts he woke up in. The clothes are old and loose and flow around him. They feel like biblical clothes, caftan-like, and as my father stands in the sunshine, his feet firmly planted in the present moment, he wonders if anyone sees him here now as he finally sees himself, as he wished to be seen for so many years in his life and wasn't—as an artist. But the lawns of the industrial park around him are deserted. No one is entering or leaving the area.

After he unwraps his brushes from the tissue paper, my father moves his easel closer to the wall of the building. He decides that, in the painting, he wants all the angles to be very abrupt. He wants the reflected building to look almost like a separate structure cocooned within the first. Watercolors as a genre are prissy, and he has to work directly against that, he thinks.

My father lights a cigarette and looks at the expansive sky. For a long time in his life, he felt ruinous. Every day he would catch more and more babies as they fell into the world and wish instead for a way to send them back. He remembers watching the nurses lower the opaque oxygen masks over laboring women's faces on his orders, and feeling the terrible sense that he was smothering them as he had been smothered, first by his father and his father's Jewish God, and then by his first family, who wailed for the good life to the point of insanity, and then, when he went bankrupt trying to give it to them, shrugged and turned their backs. But now, in Memphis, he feels something. Something much like the vacant, half-urban Tennessee country gaping open around him. He feels free.

As he works, my father loses himself in the colors and shapes of his work. Red and black. An astonishing new green. He isn't sure how much time has passed, but when he surfaces again, he looks up and notices that the windows of the building he has been painting are filled with people. They are tall and short, men and women, old and young, but they all have one thing in common—their faces are pressed against the glass, and they are, each one of them, looking at him. He's not sure why this is, but the thought occurs that it may make the painting better, scarier, and so he begins to paint the people into the watercolor, the shapes of their bodies and faces. All staring out of the skyscraper and down at him, the artist, as if they are trapped.

When the out-of-breath security guard arrives, my father is nearly finished. She is large and worried, wearing a tight sheriff's uniform, carrying a gun. "I'm sorry," she says to my father in a thick country accent, "but we've had terrorist threats. The people here would feel better" (she gestures to my father's audience in the windows) "if you would leave." The security guard turns toward the enormous parking lot and clasps her hands behind her back. "Right now."

My father is shocked. He can't believe it. Is it because of the way he's dressed? Like some kind of ruffian? Is this what the South is coming to, the whole nation? *Is this it?*

He sets down the brush and invites the guard to take a look at his rendition of the manicured grass they are both standing on. "Is there a law against painting a fucking watercolor?" he asks her, pointing at the people in the building who are still, it appears, staring down at them. "Is it because I have a goddamn *beard?*"

The guard flinches at the word, as if she has just been slapped. "I need you to evacuate the area immediately," she commands without looking at him. "Evacuate this place of business. Now."

Utterly incensed, my father slams into the Honda and burns rubber toward downtown Memphis. As he speeds away from the airport, he sees at least a dozen F-16s cruise over at a low altitude. So close to the ground he can see the markings. Feel the boom in his chest.

My father pulls off at the first freeway exit and idles for a while, waiting to see if there are more. He puts on his hazards and scans the sky for anything. Clouds. Birds. He lucked out of combat himself, but he imagines his son, who did serve in a war, would know exactly what to do in moments like this. His son would be able to tell if the silence was deadly or if it was safe. In fact, his son is probably sitting at the side of a road somewhere right now in a Honda two-door coupe just like his own. Breathing.

At one P.M. he reassembles his easel in an alley that looks out through a tangle of fire escapes and loading docks onto the cool brown ribbon of the Mississippi. He makes several attempts at the initial sketch. Then, before he realizes it, he finds himself drawing his own face when he was younger, in uniform, standing outside an army Quonset hut with his first wife, in Guam. Drawing his first wife's hair makes him laugh. He piles it higher and higher into a ridiculous pyramid, before adding in the pregnant stomach that holds his son. He places his son inside the stomach of his first wife and curls him like a caterpillar with antennae, then adds some coconut trees in the background, blowing in opposite directions, as if there is a typhoon. His oldest daughter he draws into one of the trees next, hanging by her legs from swaying branches as if she is a monkey. The youngest goes in the upper-left-hand corner, looking down at them all through a window in the ceiling, still unborn.

By two P.M. my father is tired. He drives home, steps over the newspaper, eats his lunch, lets Littleslip convince him to take a nap. They curl on the sofa together, and he dreams whatever a man dreams who is sixty and lives in Memphis with his second wife and the cat he loves. He is known to very few people, my father, but I'm sure the dreams rub up against him, purring. The bright pop and scream of a newborn in a delivery room. The lips of his humanities professor in college. Helicopter sounds.

At five-thirty he is back at the entry gate of the multinational paper conglomerate, where the kindly woman in her seventies with the American-flag toothpicks in her beehive has been replaced by several National Guardsmen wearing camouflage.

"Hey, you guys," my father jokes as he rolls down the window. "Tell me something. Do I look like a terrorist?"

Unsmiling, the men snap to attention and approach my father's vehicle. "Pardon me, sir," one of them says, leaning in toward the window. "You want to come again?"

My father gives the men an acidic look. He has just about had it with the regional South in the last twenty-four hours. The accent. The sweet tea. The naïveté.

"Is there a reason," he wonders aloud, "why representatives of the U.S. military such as themselves have been called in to protect a company whose net worth is about six hundred million rolls of toilet paper? Seriously, now. What gives?"

Shocked, the men turn to look at each other. They whistle

for reinforcements, and within seconds, a group of them have flanked the Honda. Activity comes to a standstill as my father is asked to please exit the automobile.

Once they have him out with his legs spread, the Guardsmen frisk his person in front of a half-dozen other exiting employees. My father is speechless and humiliated as the young men pat him down. He watches these uniformed children half his age open the glove compartment of the two-door, then rifle through the rest of the car and find his paints. He has left the first watercolor in the hatchback to dry, and they pull it out. The picture of the building with all the concerned faces pressed against the glass.

My father watches the group of Guardsmen examine the painting (his first audience so far), and he wonders if they like it. They seem a bit in awe of the work, even slightly upset.

"It's just people in a skyscraper," my father says. "What's the big deal?"

The one who appears to be the ringleader looks up from the picture and gazes into my father's eyes. "Jesus Christ," he says with a kind of disbelieving wonder. "Don't you know?"

The boy takes my father by the arm and escorts him to the security booth, where a portable television shows a picture of the Twin Towers of the World Trade Center in New York, one smoking, the other standing. The boy gestures at the black-and-white screen.

"There," he says, pointing, and my father watches a large jet approach the clean, upright tower and be swallowed by it in a froth of fire and glass. Abruptly, the picture changes, and he watches both buildings peel open before his eyes, blooming out and down like terrible gray flowers.

My father's hands shake as he removes his straw hat. He turns away from the screen as the pictures repeat all over again. "What the fuck is this?" he says to the young Guardsmen watching him. "What's going on?"

Several days later, I will talk to my father. He will telephone me and explain that he hasn't been able to return my repeated calls from Los Angeles because his answering machine is broken. He paid seventy dollars for it, he tells me, and he wants the money back.

"They keep asking me for the sales slip," he says. "I keep telling these assholes . . . why do I need *that?* Obviously, if I have the machine, I'm the owner. I shouldn't have to prove anything."

It was a national emergency, I want to tell him, there are pay phones. But I keep my mouth shut.

We exchange stories of where we were when it happened. I tell him how his first wife, my mother, called from Oregon at seven-thirty in the morning, screaming into the answering machine: "There are bombs."

He talks about the U.S. carriers that made nuisances of themselves off the coast of Yemen, and then the plots of his favorite films. *Zabriskie Point. The Passenger,* starring Jack Nicholson. "That city is hell on people," he says about New York. "So dangerous."

"It was my home, remember?" I tell my father. "I lived there for eleven years. In 1993, when the first bombs went off under the Trade Center, I was on a train that stalled under Chambers Street. From the force of the rumbling, and the smoke back at Cortlandt, we all knew it was something bad."

My father pauses at this, and his voice fades. When I lived in New York, we weren't talking, and we both know it. Those were the Manhattan years, when an impenetrable, spiraling silence rose up between us. A vast concrete island of resentment. Stories high. Blocks long.

"Nicholson's a brilliant actor," my father says quietly. "Just so good."

We are silent now, and I look out the window at the curtains of light coming down on Los Angeles. It is garbage day tomorrow, and the cans are lined up evenly along the street.

"Should go, Dad," I say, imagining his cat in his lap, his living room in Memphis I have not ever seen. "Talk to you later." But my father doesn't hang up. He begins to speak, then stops midsentence. I wonder for a minute if he hasn't dropped the phone. When his voice comes on the line again, it is delicate, too fragile, almost, to recognize.

"I was so worried about you when you were little," he says. "I couldn't even stand it when you had to go out to sell Campfire candy. I couldn't stand to let you even walk out the door."

THE HEIGHTS

Whenever my mother is drunk and in the company of men, she likes to get going on old dental-school stories about Daddy. This is usually on the afternoon of a Monday when the house is closed to the people who pay money to see it, and most probably in the springtime, when whatever doctor she's been courting will come over for drinks with some of his other doctor friends after their golf game out at Edgewater or Vernonia.

Roundabout happy hour is when they show. Tires squealing up the cobble drive that snakes to the top of our front lawn. From Daddy's bay window, I'll watch them pull in. Nudging the snouts of their Town Cars and Cougars up as close to the front entrance as they possibly can. And even from three stories up, on the other side of brick walls and thick double glass, I can hear them. Bursting into the foyer without bothering to use the knocker. A horde of mix-and-match plaid and laughing good nature, smelling up the place with cigar smoke and fresh grass cuttings. Calling out my mother's name, which is Natalie.

"Natalie, Natalie," they'll chorus, charging toward the sitting room bar, cracking ice into Opa's crystal tumblers, popping handfuls of pearl onions and green olives into their mouths straight from the jars. And one or two of them, like Dr. Al Kraft or Dr. Jimmie Zerr, who are from The Heights and know my mother better from childhood, might even climb halfway up to the second floor.

"Natty," they'll shout from the landing. "You indescribable bitch."

And I know she can hear them just as well from her own room, too, yanking open all the curtain sash cords with dirty hands, catcalling like a bunch of teenagers on their way back down.

This is the old family place we have to live in now. Full of Oma's rickety antiques and echoes and whispering sunlight trying to get in. And for those men who've never been here before, for those who might have had to work their own way through med school, they always manage to get awed by something. My mother is a Dosch whose great-grandmother was a Biedermann, and when Oregon Trail settlers first came to Hillsboro along the John Day, it was her relatives who put them to work.

"It's just mine on paper," she'll say to visitors from the Historical Society or the Collector's Armory, shrugging a little when they compliment her on this or that view of Mount Hood from the north windows or the oval duck pond out back that Opa dug all by himself. "Just mine on paper," she'll murmur, staring down at her hands and twisting her rings. "But what really belongs to us, anyway?"

Some of the doctors, if they are still married, will use our telephone first thing to call their wives, and there might be some debating over which one of Daddy's jazz records to put on the stereo. But my mother will never come down for that. She will stay put in her bedroom until they are all poured and settled, the ice jingling in their glasses. And when all their after-sport energy has slowed to a gentle, even buzz, and it's as if they might have forgotten already why they are all here in the first place, I will sneak to the second floor and hide in the stairwell next to the elevator, waiting for my mother's door to brush lightly against the carpet. From there I'll watch the sidling rustle of her descent. Sometimes she'll pause at the bottom of the stairs, on the other side of the archway leading into the sitting room. She'll lean her back against the wall, holding her glass, cool and sweating, against the side of her throat, and she'll listen to them all talking over one another, swaying a little to the Peggy Lee they might have chosen or the Connie Boswell, the Anita O'Day.

Sometimes I'll watch her wait like that for five, ten, even fifteen minutes before going in to the men, and at those times, when she's quiet, when she's standing there, waiting for just the right moment to make her entrance, I'll almost choke on my breath from the sight of her, although I can't say why. Red cloisonné lips, and skin powdered Kabuki white. Leaning back against the door in one of Oma's embroidered robes over her fancy spearmint-silk pajamas, the cigarette smoke streaming out her mouth and nose. Most times she doesn't even know I'm there, but if she does happen to catch me, watching her from the shadows at the top of the stairs, she'll signal for me to wait. Wait until the coast is clear before bringing Daddy down. And although it would be easy, I suppose, to step in and defy her, this is a request I always honor, though as I mentioned, I can't say why.

This Monday, for some reason unbeknownst to me, the foursome arrives a little early. Daddy's nurse has just barely gone home, and when I wheel him past the party room about an hour later, planning to sneak him out for the afternoon walk as I always do, my mother overhears.

"Liz," she says, her voice high and excited, as if she knows she's about to make everybody laugh. "Honey, come in here, will you?"

"Can't right now," I call from the foyer. "I'm on the way out."

Loud whispers fill the party room, and after a minute, my mother appears in the doorway, floating toward us like a wraith in one of Oma's white linen suits.

"It's all right, baby," she says, brushing off the shoulders of the blue sport coat Daddy's nurse always dresses him in for his daily walk. "Why don't both of you join us?"

She is speaking loudly enough for every human being in the vicinity to hear that I'm not alone, but my mother doesn't seem to register my disbelief.

"Stop it," I mouth, pointing at Daddy, "what are you doing?" and this makes her come to me. It makes her reach over Daddy and fluff the front of my hair.

"Please, Liz," she whispers. "It's just Al and Jimmie. Just Al and Jimmie, and two other new friends they met out at Oswego. I was telling them all about you."

"You weren't."

"Oh, yes, I was so," she says, kissing the top of my head. "Because you're splendid. Both you and Daddy. So don't worry about it now. Come on in."

But I do worry, of course, and when the three of us enter, my mother leading, then me behind, pushing Daddy, Dr. Al gives us a giant round of applause.

"Hey, look at you, Lizzie," he says, winking at me from behind the bar, where my mother has put him to work mixing up her champagne cocktails. "What a beauty."

I freeze, hoping his focus on me will be brief, but it's like a flashlight pointed directly into my eyes.

"Don't be embarrassed, sweetie," says Dr. Al, who happens to be sporting one of Opa's nautical hats. "It's the truth."

"Dear God," my mother says to the room. "Will you listen to that? No fool like an old fool, right, everybody?"

"You bet your ass," says Dr. Al. "Bring that daughter over here."

My mother stiffens as the room erupts in laughter. "In your dreams, Buddy," she answers, sliding an arm around my shoulders and turning me—even though my hands are still locked around the handles on the back of Daddy's chair—away from Dr. Al at the bar and toward the center of the room, where Dr. Jimmie and two other scrubbed-looking younger ones with Kaiser Permanente stitched onto their red golf sweaters are leaning back on the sofa, trying not to stare openly at the condition of my father.

"And here are the fabulous Klipsch brothers," my mother says, waving a hand toward the two sweaters. "They're dentists, if you can believe it. And twins."

"Not twins, actually," one of them corrects her, smiling. "Just brothers."

"Well, they play like twins," says Dr. Jimmie, sucking at the fresh end of a new cigar. "Wasn't one hole the jokers didn't bogey on the back nine."

This gets a big hoot from everybody, and when it dies down, my mother returns to the introductions.

"This is my daughter, Elisabeth-Gail," she says to the two sweaters, gathering my hair up into a side ponytail, then letting it drop. "In the fall she'll be at the Oregon Health Sciences on accelerated entry, the only freshman in the whole class they picked like that, right, honey?"

I put my hand on Daddy's shoulder as if I haven't heard her, and there is a thick, squirming hush as all the eyes in the room move over me, wavering somewhere between warm and expectant, even edging a bit toward resentful.

"So, med school all the way, huh?" one of the sweaters says to me at last, breaking the silence, and before I can get to answering, the whole room nods in unison.

"That's right," my mother answers, moving toward Dr. Al at

the bar with her empty glass outstretched. "No scraping dirty yellow teeth for my daughter. She'll be a surgeon, just like he and Jimmie are. All blood and guts."

"A cardiologist," I explain to the Klipsch brother who asked. "If I make it."

"If she makes it," my mother says. "Will you listen to that? You should see what she reads, this girl. Medical books with people who have their faces smushed in tractor accidents. I can't even look at it."

"Well, OHS is damn good," says the other sweater, who hasn't spoken up thus far, his eyes steady on the front of my blouse. "Mazel tov."

"Thanks," I say, and Dr. Al starts tapping his class ring against the neck of the bitters bottle. "Are you hearing this, Z?" he calls to Dr. Jimmie. "OHS on accelerated entry. You get to needing the emphysema tank? Here's the girl that can hook you up."

"Quiet now, you," my mother says to Dr. Al, sipping long from the new drink he's handed her. "Jimmie has to stick around to take care of me."

"My pleasure, darling," Dr. Jimmie says, putting his stocking feet up on the new glass coffee table. "But Kraft will be sewing me closed long before that. I'm going full-on arterio."

"You're very bad, both of you," my mother says to them. "There's someone else our new friends need to meet."

My mother motions me from the bar to bring Daddy over, and when I surrender him to her, she steps around Dr. Al and puts a hand on Daddy's loose cheek.

"And this," she announces to the Klipsch brothers, "is Cass. My husband, the oral surgeon. As we can see, he has had a fit."

"A stroke," I correct her. "Cerebral embolism."

"Bingo," Dr. Jimmie says to me. "A-plus," and both the Klipsch brothers bob their heads at Daddy politely. This they get.

"He's looking pretty good today, though," Dr. Al says to my mother. "Decent, don't you think?"

"Al-l-l," she sighs, drawing out his name. "Please."

"Well, I think he does look good, Natty," Dr. Al says. "And I'm his doctor, for chrissake."

"Come on now, Mommy and Dad," Dr. Jimmie says. "No fighting."

My mother tips her head back at Dr. Jimmie as if she's about to laugh, but no sound comes out. Her eyes lock on Dr. Al's, and his stay on hers while Daddy rests in between them like a piece of land, a large quiet territory they are vying for.

"I'm going," I say, "before it gets dark."

"Good idea," Dr. Al says, removing my mother's hands from the handles of Daddy's wheelchair and pushing him toward me. "Let's send the lovely young thing on her way."

"Pleasure to meet you," I say, nodding toward the Klipsch brothers, but my mother's hand on my shoulder doesn't loosen.

"Albert," she says, holding me in place and pressing her face next to mine. "Which lovely young thing do you mean?" She bats her eyelashes, daring him to change the course of the afternoon, but Dr. Al backs down.

"I mean you, dumbbell," he says, beaming down at her, then out toward the room. "And that deserves a toast."

Jimmie shrugs, and the Klipsch brothers try not to glance at Daddy. They raise their glasses at each other and waggle the ice.

"Natty," Dr. Al says, "come over here right now, and bring me your glass." He crooks his finger at her sweetly, but my mother ignores him, setting her glass down on the end table beside us, out of his reach.

"You know," she says, abandoning the bar and striding over to the sofa, where she wedges herself in between Dr. Jimmie and the two sweaters. "I love having dentists around. Dentists are sexy, aren't they?"

"You bet," Dr. Jimmie says, but my mother covers his mouth with her finger. "No, Dolly," she says, smiling. "I want you to ask Al."

Dr. Jimmie shakes his head and groans, covering his heart as if it's broken. "Al, Al, always Al. What do you think, Kraft? Are dentists sexy?"

"You put your hands in people's mouths all the time, Jimmie," Dr. Al says. "It's pretty exotic."

"Bet these two Kaiser boys have some stories, though," Dr. Jimmie says to my mother, sliding his arm along the back of the sofa behind her shoulders.

"That we do," says one of the sweaters, glancing up at me. "But not in mixed company."

"Shit," my mother says, resting the back of her head on Dr. Jimmie's arm. "Do I look like a nun? Before I married Cass, I certainly used to act like one. Al remembers. Right, Al? Why don't you ask the brothers K if they want to hear about you and Cass out at the Scappoose Airfield?"

Dr. Al sets down one of his bottles mid-pour and stares at the foursome on the couch, his face perfectly still.

"Uh-oh," Dr. Jimmie says, grinning over at Dr. Al. "I haven't heard about that one."

"Of course you haven't, Boo Boo," says my mother, patting Dr. Jimmie's thick waist. "You were too busy setting a good example."

"Oh, that," says Dr. Jimmie. "Yeah, right."

"Natalie," Dr. Al says, looking over at Daddy and me. "Come on."

"Oh, buzz off," my mother says, lifting Jimmie's empty glass above her head and tapping on it with a fingernail. "I want to tell these boys and my daughter about the day Cass flew you home from Vegas. You've never heard this one, have you, Liz?"

The room turns in the direction of the bar, and I feel my face get hot. "No."

"Don't mumble, honey. What did you say?"

"I said I've heard a lot of stories."

"That's right," my mother says, leaning toward the Klipsch brother closest to her. "She has. But not this one. Anyway, Cass over there and Al, they both graduated school the same year. Nineteen hundred and seventy-six. Dental and med, respectively."

"Hear, hear," the sweaters intone.

"Do me a favor, Lizzie," Dr. Al says to me, running his thumb around the rim of his drink. "Go for your walk."

"Albert," my mother says, standing and turning to the bar. "My daughter is eighteen years old. She doesn't just run and do what you say."

My mother's eyes leave Dr. Al's and settle on me. "Well?" she says.

But outside, the daylight is fading, blackening the sharp rock edges of Opa's duck pond, and I can imagine a hundred things that could go wrong for Daddy and me out there in the dark.

"It's too late," I say quietly, avoiding Dr. Al's gaze. "Never mind."

"You see that, party pooper?" my mother says, smiling up at him. "My daughter, darling, not yours. And take off that ridiculous hat."

"I will not," Dr. Al says, and the two bottles he's holding clink together hard as he tosses them back in the empty ice bucket. "Pick another story."

"Hell no, Kraft," Dr. Jimmie says. "I want to hear it."

"And you will," my mother says, turning her back on Dr. Al and again settling down in between Dr. Jimmie and the Klipsch brothers. "So here were Cass and Al, right? Top of their class, or up near enough to it, and that was a grand occasion. You remember your own graduation, right?" she asks the young men.

"That was it," the Klipsch brothers agree. "A party."

"Exactly," my mother continues, sliding her feet up on the coffee table next to Dr. Jimmie's. "Except I was way, way too pregnant with Liz to go on any kind of a bender. So my parents, the ones who built this house we're all sitting in right now, they chartered a private plane and sent Cassie and Al to Las Vegas for the weekend with a blank check, if you can believe it. To just go wild."

"Those were the days of wine and roses," Dr. Jimmie says, tipping his drink glass toward Daddy. "How much the Dosch Foundation lose on that bright lightbulb? Nobody raged like Cass."

"This goes without saying," my mother says. "Which is exactly why he's sitting over there like a sea vegetable. Anyway, these two were set loose upon Nevada for three nights, two days, and when we went out to the Scappoose Airfield to pick them up—my mother and father, Oma and Opa Dosch, and their sweet knocked-up daughter, Natalie, right? All dressed up. Ready to go greet their son-in-law and his best friend, the two conquering heroes here, they come stumbling off the plane too drunk to stand up. Al, over there, he practically falls halfway down the stairs."

"Is this a story or what, Natty?" Dr. Jimmie asks. "Where's the beef?"

"Jimmie," my mother says, covering his mouth again. "Stop."

"Can I get a little refill from you, buddy?" one of the Klipsch brothers calls over to the bar. "Anything."

"Got you covered," Dr. Al says, giving them a thumbs-up, but when the sweaters look away, I notice Dr. Al stare into the liquor cabinet and not reach for a thing.

"So, you get this pretty picture, right?" my mother asks the rest of the group.

"Loud and clear," answer the two Klipsches.

"Well, super-duper," she says, applauding their effort. "Circus-Circus. So here they come, stumbling up to us, Cass and Al, and behind them is this little girl. This little Vietnamese girl in spike heels. 'Surprise,' Cass says to me, pushing this little thing forward, his voice slurring all over the place. 'This is Lorelei.'"

"Son of a bitch," Dr. Jimmie says. "Hooker, right?"

"Bingo," says my mother, but when she and Dr. Jimmie turn to Dr. Al for confirmation, his face is almost as blank and numb-looking as Daddy's.

"Oh, come on, Allie," my mother calls over her shoulder. "You want to tell these boys her name?"

"An effing hooker," Dr. Jimmie says, shaking his head.

"But that's not all there is," says my mother. "Not with Cass. Cassie drapes Al's arm around this girl's skinny little shoulders and, on cue, Al starts squeezing her tight." 'Here she is, Natty,' Albert says to me. 'I'd like you to meet Mrs. Lorelei Kraft.'"

"Well, what do you know," says Dr. Jimmie. "Al married himself a whore."

"Well, no, Jimmie," my mother says, winking at the Klipsch brothers. "No. We're in mixed company here. Let's be nice. Let's use 'hostess' or 'escort' or 'lady of the evening.'"

"I like that one," Dr. Jimmie says, looking over my mother's head at the Klipsch brothers. "'Lady of the evening,' what do you think?"

"Jesus," says the Klipsch brother nearest my mother, looking down at his own checkered knees.

"Right," my mother says. "Well, apparently, our Cassie made a bet with Al or slipped him a mickey or God knows what all else to get him to go down the aisle. You know Al. Dr. One Night Stand. And of course, this is right at the end of the war, so my father is not so happy at all about this specimen's nationality. Not at all. Who cares that she's a lady of the evening, right? He's clenching his jaw so hard it looks like he'll shatter his teeth because she's Vietnamese.

"And can I tell you about my mother? She's about to evaporate right off the runway, and I'm so precious and virginal back in those days, I start crying. Buckets, and I mean hard. I start having a fucking fit, but my parents are still standing there like it's a receiving line at the cotillion, craning their heads around, hoping no one is looking."

"And were they?" Dr. Jimmie asks, stubbing out the end of his cigar. "I sure as hell would've been."

"I don't even remember," my mother says. "But halfway through this tantrum, I start beating Cass around the face with my fists as hard as I can. My own mother has to set down her purse for a minute to try and get me off him, but it doesn't do any good. Cass is so drunk it's like hitting a wet wrestling mat. But you see, by this time, I'm actually getting to like it. So then I start hitting Al, too, and after a minute Cass starts trying to defend himself, and he kind of halfway slaps me across the face. Well, it's limp, and it doesn't even hurt, but this makes my father jump into it. So finally, it's just my mother and Mrs. Lorelei Kraft standing there on the runway."

"Excellent," says Dr. Jimmie. "Love American-style."

"Exactly," my mother says. "And that marriage lasted about five entire minutes. In the end, my mother had to drive our new pal Lorelei to the bus. And can't you imagine it? My Oma at the Greyhound station with this chippie in her pink shantung shoes? Helping her buy the ticket back to Sin City? I don't think I ever saw my mother driving herself anywhere except for that day. I can see it, though, Oma trying to be polite, pointing out all the sights along the way. Welcome to the Rose City. Because really. This poor thing, right? She comes all the way to Portland thinking she's landed the big one, and all she gets to see is I-5 between Scappoose and downtown."

By now the sweaters are starting to fidget. They are looking over at the bar for their drinks that never came, holding their watches out to each other, tapping on the faces. "Pretty late, bro," I can hear them saying to themselves. "Gotta fly."

But they stay, sinking deeper into Opa's comfortable furniture. They ask my mother what happened.

"Oh, I don't know," she says, brushing off the front of her suit. "We did the paperwork and got rid of her. Didn't we, darling?"

Dr. Al's hand trembles as he adjusts the brim of Opa's hat. "Cass is the one who took care of that, Natalie," he says. "My best friend."

"What's that?" my mother asks, rising off the couch. "What did you just say?"

She puts her hands on her hips, waiting for an answer, but Dr. Al stares past her, out the leaded glass window.

"Hey," my mother says sharply, and I see him flinch. "Cassie never left a thumbprint on that bimbo."

"Why not, Natty?" Dr. Al murmurs, still gazing outside at the river lights. "It was a blank check."

Dr. Jimmie's stocking feet slide off the coffee table to the floor, and the room turns to focus on my mother, who, instead of being extinguished by Dr. Al, seems to be glowing even brighter, like a giant night moth in Oma's white linen suit.

"You know what, Al, you big wet blanket?" she snaps, nabbing the brothers' empty glasses in one clean sweep. "Even now, he's twice the man you are. Nobody else will ever come close."

She starts toward the bar, swirling ice, but before she arrives, Dr. Al's shoulders hunch, then cringe a little, and he puts his fingers up to the bridge of his nose and pushes hard, in a way that looks like it hurts.

It should have taken Dr. Jimmie and the Klipsch brothers no time at all to grab their shoes and get out, three or four minutes at most, probably. But their reflexes seem all slowed down. It could have been Opa's good liquor that held them in place. Or simple embarrassment.

Maybe, like me, they have never seen a man cry. Although

Daddy's nurse says he does that sometimes. Sometimes water will squeeze out the sides of his eyes when he's lying on his back. She calls it crying, and even though I read in my survey on neurological dysfunction that this can just be from pressure, they are not actual tears, I don't correct Daddy's nurse when she treats them as if they're real. I think the tears Dr. Al is shedding now must be pressure of a similar kind. So I leave Daddy by himself, and I go to Dr. Al. I step around my mother and place my hand over both the hands he operates with. I hold them there. The skin under my palm is hot and dry and chapped-feeling, and as soon as I touch him, he closes his eyes.

"You'll be a good one," he says to me, interlacing our fingers. "A good one, Lizzie."

"Oh, heavenly Christ," my mother sighs. "Elisabeth, stop."

And even though I know that gestures of this kind are pointless—that I will never be capable of becoming a doctor, that I will see Dr. Al even as soon as tomorrow morning, standing in the pantry in his sleepover robe while my mother moves up and slips her arms around him from behind when they think the maid isn't looking—I leave my fingers curled in between Dr. Al's. "I'm sorry," I want to tell him. "I'm sorry that you love us."

By the Time
You Get This

M y husband and I live in Los Angeles near a large reservoir. We're in the hills, set back from the road. All you can see when you look out the windows is water. When she was small, our daughter used to call it the ocean.

Every morning at dawn, I stand at the kitchen window and watch my husband jog around the edge of the reservoir. It's dark when he starts out, but the light fills in around him quickly, seeping up the canyon walls and into the water like blood.

These days my husband's legs are well defined, and he runs easily. His stomach is hard and flat. Today he's in gym shorts and the same ratty T-shirt he used to wear when I met him in the East Village back in medical school. I drink coffee and stare at the treetops, the unearthly blue of the water. The last time we were in bed together, it bothered me to look at him, he was in such good shape. I had to turn out the lights right away.

When he comes in this morning, he is on the headset, in midconversation with one of the Realtors. He takes the towel I left out for him, kisses the side of my face, and walks past me into the den. I pour more coffee and stay at the window. Since he put the house on the market last week, there are Realtors on the phone every time it rings. I see them cruising by the house during business hours when they think we're gone, craning their necks out of unmarked cars. My husband's voice is muffled in the other room, but the tone is adamant. *We want to move on this.* I hear him hang up without saying goodbye, then pick up a land line and call his sports broker in New York.

My husband buys, sells, and collects athletic memorabilia. He has been doing it since our daughter entered high school five years ago. Some of the most valuable things are displayed in a small gallery he has created for them downstairs. At first expanding the collection was something he and our daughter did together sometimes after school and on weekends. When they started, it was all the two of them ever talked about, but as time went on, she lost interest.

When his broker picks up, my husband moves to the door between us and gently slides it shut. Outside on the deck, the hot tub is covered with a black tarp and a thick layer of pine needles. I close my eyes. This winter there has been sun for 130 days in a row. Right now there is not one cloud. The water and sky reflect each other. Two blue plates. I leave the sweat from my husband's kiss where it is. On the side of my face, it stings and prickles as it dries.

I can't explain why I wrote the note when I did. I was just sitting in my office last summer, and it appeared on the back of a prescription pad. *Dear Rob, I don't love you anymore.* Then I signed my full name.

For most of my adult life, I was a practicing psychiatrist, but I couldn't think of any better way to put it. When I was finished, I folded the note and put it in the pocket of the jacket I wore to see clients. Then I shut off the lights and went to another part of the house.

Lately, when my husband is back from running or just out of the shower, he wonders if he made the right choice to sell the house. "We need to do this now, don't we?" he says. "Don't you think?" But he knows how I feel about it. When I tell him that wasn't our agreement, he can barely look me in the eye.

After my husband goes upstairs, I brew more coffee and watch the rest of our neighbors jog around the reservoir. The movie star, the studio executive, the body builder. They wear the same-style sweatsuit with variations. As they pass around the curve at the base of our driveway, I see them glance up at the house. From the high angle of the window, it looks as if their feet are barely touching the ground.

Our housekeeper was the one who found the note I had written. Her name is Lydia. She comes on Tuesdays, sometimes more often if I ask her. Lydia is from El Salvador and wears sweatshirts that say *Crapped Out: Las Vegas!* and *I love Grandma*. I feel guilty making her do all the cleaning now that I'm not working, so lately, we've been rotating several of the tasks.

When Lydia brought me the note, I was on my hands and knees, vacuuming the hair off the dog's bed. She touched my shoulder and I jumped.

"Why you write this?" she said, shoving the paper at me. The vacuum was roaring between us.

"You shouldn't walk up behind people like that," I said. "It scares them half to death."

Lydia stared down at me in disbelief. Physically, she is a small person, but Lydia has the demeanor of a general. I leaned over and turned off the vacuum cleaner.

Lydia shook her head. "This is very bad." She spoke to the note as if it were responsible. "I tell you something, Mrs. Lady," she said. "Dr. Rob is good. He is a good, good man."

I stood up and brushed off my pants. "Why were you looking through my things?"

Lydia didn't answer. She balled up the note, stuck it in the vacuum-cleaner hose, and turned it back on. The vacuum cleaner hiccuped, and the note disappeared into its depth.

"There." Lydia put her hands on my shoulders, and her face was right next to mine. "You listen," she said. "You stop right now. This is a gloomy house. No wonder."

After what seems like a long time, my husband appears in his suit and tie and feeds the dog. I'm still standing at the window. The coffee is cold in my hand.

"Tell Lydia goodbye for me, can you?"

I nod.

"We'll miss her, won't we, you know that, right?" He stands behind me with his arms around my waist, and we listen to our daughter's dog eat, its tags and collar clinking against the bowl. He rests his chin on my shoulder. "Somebody made an offer, you know. Sight unseen. The agent wants to bring someone over in a few hours, and I told him you'll show them around. You'll do that, right?"

When I turn to look at him, my husband sighs. "It's been over a year now."

I move to pour out the coffee, but he won't let go of my shoulder.

"How long have you been standing here?" he asks. "Mary?"

I think I answer him: "Not long." I mean to, anyway, but when I turn around, he's gone, and I can't see his car on the road. Just other houses and other mailboxes. And trees.

I set out the garbage bags for Lydia and do the dishes for her. Then I change the head of the damp mop and strip the beds. Our daughter's room is at the end of the hall. The clean sheets I put on the bed a week ago are pink and peel back from the mattress like skin. The grief counselor said it was better to take down the things in the room or rearrange them. To not make a shrine. But I don't know which is better: to have to look at her things every day or to know they're in the closet in boxes. So far I haven't been able to decide.

Lydia is the one who found our daughter, she and her grown son Paul, who is developmentally challenged and comes with her to work sometimes. My husband and I were away, attending a cardiology conference in Palm Springs. We were there because Rob invented a small tube that is essential to heart transplants. He is not a doctor, my husband, only an inventor, but his work has been mentioned in several textbooks. Our daughter once did a report on him for school.

We were at the opening ceremonies of the conference in a large auditorium when the call came in. My husband was the keynote speaker. He was standing at the podium in front of seventeen hundred people when the girl from the concierge station came to my seat with the note.

Emergency at home, it said. *Please call Lydia.*

Since it happened, I've been paying Lydia more and more. At first it was five extra a week, then ten, twenty. In the beginning Lydia didn't say anything to me about the money, but later, she starting leaving it in obvious places for me to find. She also returned the space heater I had given her and some linens. At that point she hadn't quit, but I knew she'd been thinking about it. Then, two weeks ago, she arrived with a priest.

"This is Father Sandoval," she said. "He wants to bless the house."

I excused myself and sat in my office while they prayed together in Spanish. The door was open, and I could hear the words moving slowly through the halls. It took forty-five minutes, then Lydia came and tapped on my door. "It's done now, Mrs. Lady," she said. "And don't pay me for today, either."

Lydia told the police that when she and Paul entered the

house, the first thing they saw was our daughter in the hot tub. Lydia told them that my daughter was sitting in the water fully dressed, staring into the kitchen as if she was alive.

After it happened, my husband and I agreed that we couldn't think about selling the house. We didn't want the Realtors coming by with the potential buyers, having to answer their questions. By law, you have to alert people to the history of a property. They could sue us if we didn't, my husband said.

One day I imagine I will slit the black covering open with a knife, and she'll be alive in the bottom of the hot tub. I imagine I'll let her out then, and she will be a year older. As the anniversary nears, I wait for the feel of that knife, slicing through the thick skin of the tarp, for the quick intake of breath, the gasp, as my daughter's head shoots up from the depths.

"Jesus, Mommy," she'll say, climbing out of the water in her angry black clothes. "Took you long enough."

Lydia first announced she was leaving the week after Father Sandoval came. "You can do without me" was how she put it. "Just a couple Tuesdays more and I quit."

When she told me, I stopped sorting laundry and stood with my back to her for a long time. "It's all right," I said. "You go home now. I'll finish up."

Later, when my husband arrived and found me cleaning the bathroom, he was upset. He knelt down on the tiles and pulled the toilet brush out of my hand. "I want you to stand up right now, Mary," he said. "I mean it. There are plenty of people we can hire to clean a house."

The following Tuesday, Lydia and I worked on separate floors until it was time for her to go. When I was finished, I found her in the kitchen, sterilizing the cleaning gloves at the sink. She had the lights out, and all the blinds were closed against the sun.

"You know what, Mrs. Lady?" she said without turning around. "I take you next week to meet my niece."

I stood in the doorway watching Lydia's back. "Why is that?"

"Oh, I don't know," Lydia said. "She gives readings for people. My niece has a gift."

I sat down at the table and wrote out Lydia's check. The amount of bleach she was using made it difficult to breathe. "I don't see psychics," I said.

"Okay," Lydia said. "But you'll be glad to go. My niece is a seer. I give you a present."

"I don't need a present from you, Lydia." I tore out the check and wrote the number in the ledger. "I think you should stay."

Lydia came to the table and sat down across from me. The light from the deck was glowing around the edges of the window frames.

"Where will you go if you don't work here?" I asked. "Do you have another job?"

Lydia looked away as I handed her the check. "It's late now, Mrs. Lady," she said. "I gotta go now and get my son."

I told the grief counselor, "Why would I make a shrine out of a teenager's room? It was a mess." On the way out, the grief counselor tried to hand me a book on death and dying. "That won't be necessary," my husband said. "My wife is a psychiatrist."

"That's ridiculous," I said to my husband and grabbed the book out of the counselor's hand. The following week, when it came time for our appointment, the grief counselor didn't arrive and didn't call. My husband and I waited in the dining room for her for two hours. Then he went jogging, and I made arrangements to send the book back to the address on her card.

This morning the bus brings Lydia at ten. She arrives in a black raincoat with several pounds of tangerines in a net. Paul trails after her like a shadow with his transistor radio, humming to himself. I've never been quite sure what is wrong with Paul, exactly, if he is autistic or mildly retarded, and I haven't asked. He is at least fifty pounds overweight, but his movements are strangely graceful, like those of a large panda.

After they found our daughter, Lydia says Paul didn't want to come back to the house for a long time, but he seems to have gotten over it. Sometimes he'll be in the kitchen and just point out at the deck without saying a word. It angers Lydia when he does this, and she slaps his hand down. Other times, when Lydia is upstairs working and I'm downstairs with Paul alone, I have found him standing outside the locked door at the end of the hall, tapping on it lightly, calling her name.

"Yes, Paul," I'll say to him. "Sarah."

"Hello, everybody," Lydia says carefully, to the kitchen more than to me. "Here we come." She peels off Paul's coat while he's still in midstride, then settles him in a chair.

This morning the back of Paul's hair is still in a whorl from the pillow. There are bread crumbs in the corner of his mouth. Lydia slices a hole in the mesh bag with her penknife and takes out one of the tangerines. "*Cuidado,*" she says as she hands it to him. "Don't make a mess."

I watch Paul remove the skin, then I go to him and kiss the top of his head. His hair is thin and fine and smells alive.

"Hi, Mary," he says.

"You drink too much," Lydia says, pointing to the coffee machine. "Too much."

I pour some for her, and she sits down. "Listen, you," she says, grabbing my wrist when I set the cup in front of her. "Bones. You can't live on that."

I smile. "Don't you notice how clean this house is?"

Lydia looks around and nods. "Okay," she says, letting go of my arm. "But you need to get ready. My niece says ten-thirty."

I try to explain that my husband doesn't want us to go this

morning, that he has invited people to come to the house, but Lydia doesn't budge.

"What people?" she says, crossing her arms. "Who?"

"I didn't tell you we'd go," I say. "I told you we'd see."

Lydia doesn't answer. Silently, she reaches for a wet nap and begins to wipe Paul's face and hands.

"Dr. Rob is counting on me today," I tell her. "I made a promise."

Lydia ignores me and continues to wipe around her son's clean mouth. "Mrs. Lady, we're going to do it," she says as she finishes. "After that you're gonna let me quit."

When we drove home from Palm Springs, the 10 had construction, so we cut across San Jacinto, through Idyllwild. My husband drove fast and talked to Lydia on the phone. The mountain roads were lined with broken white boulders that looked like pieces of the moon.

"Sit down and don't move," he told her. "I mean it. Let the people do their jobs."

Before we left for the weekend, my daughter was sitting near the hot tub with one of her vampire books, smoking. "Take care, Mommy," she called when I knocked on the window to tell her to put it out. "Don't let Dr. Robbie make a fool of himself."

As we drove up to the house, we saw the ambulance parked in front of the garage. There was a cluster of neighbors standing at the bottom of the drive. Some of them hugged me. My husband went on ahead. The ambulance lights were throbbing on and off. Our back door was open, and I could hear people inside, talking into radios. Then I looked up and saw the gurney on the deck.

After I change my shirt, I put the dog in the kennel and disarm the security system for the Realtors. There is a loud click, then a beep that releases the alarm on the front door. I leave a note saying to come in, then walk to the end of the hall and stand in the doorway of my daughter's room. With the blinds drawn, it looks like a museum of all the projects she started and didn't finish. Her brief stint with photography and acrylics, with fine-papermaking and graphic design. I imagine the buyers cycling through with the agent, whispering to each other as they finger the empty ashtrays, the even stack of books. My shoes leave indentations on the clean carpet as I go to my daughter's stereo and turn it on just loud enough for them to hear. Then I shut the door, and I lock it from the outside.

Down in the garage, Lydia and Paul are waiting patiently next to the car.

"If we go to see your niece," I tell her, "you can't quit right away. Deal?"

Lydia's hand tightens on the bag of tangerines. She stares at the hood of the car and doesn't answer.

"All right, then," I say. "What if we decide on it afterward? What about that?"

Lydia gestures for me to get in. "We'll see." She helps Paul into the passenger seat and buckles him up.

"You can listen to the big radio, Paul," I tell him, but he shakes his head and stiffens.

I haven't opened my side of the garage in quite some time, and the door struggles as it rises, creaking, like the drawbridge on a moat. I feel a little dazed by the rush of green and sun, but I step on the gas, and the car charges down the driveway, unnoticed by any of the neighbors who keep an eye on us now that we are the local rumor. At the bottom of the canyon, I glance in the rearview mirror at Lydia and find her looking back at me.

"What?" I ask. "What's the matter?"

"Nothing," she says. "You're driving good. Slow down."

When I walked into the house from Palm Springs, Lydia was surrounded by police. When she saw me come in, she ran to me, then stopped before I could touch her. I held out my arms, but she wouldn't come any closer. "I'm sorry," I told Lydia, "so sorry," but she just looked at me in that moment as if she had been slapped. I dropped my arms to my sides and held them there. Then she ran to my husband, and he held her while she cried.

Before Lydia found my daughter, we got along well. She told me stories of her life and Paul's. I would pick her up at home in Echo Park and drive her back there. She didn't take the bus. In those days, Lydia would come into my office when she knew I wasn't with clients and sit across from me on the couch. She would look around the room and nod approvingly at my certificates.

"So, Mrs. Lady," she'd say. "Go ahead. Fix my problems."

Half an hour later, we pull up in front of a peach stucco apartment building off Electric Avenue in Venice. It's on the side of the street with lower property values, but still, it's a bright place, with wind chimes in the archway and twin rubber trees growing up to meet each other over the door. I wait as Lydia untangles Paul, and while she isn't looking, I take out my phone and dial my husband's office. As it rings, I feel prepared to explain myself, but when the receptionist comes on, I can't speak. I cannot begin to tell my husband that I have abandoned the house, that I have driven across town to see our ex-housekeeper's niece who is purported to be psychic. These are simply not words he would understand.

I lock the car, and the three of us make our way into the building. The hallways are deserted, but as we climb the stairs, I can hear voices speaking Spanish inside the walls, echoing behind doors.

At the third-floor landing, Paul forges ahead, and we follow him toward a small courtyard apartment at the end of the hall.

"*Buenas,*" Lydia calls out, "happy good morning," and an

attractive, tousled-looking young woman in jeans and a T-shirt appears at the door. As soon as I lay eyes on her, I hesitate, but Lydia hooks my elbow and guides me into the tiny foyer.

"Here she is," Lydia says brightly. "My niece who I tell you about. Luz Maria. Pretty, right? What did I say?"

"Hi, Lucy," Paul calls out, "Lucy, Lucy, Lucy—"

"Quiet," Lydia says, yanking his sleeve, but the niece laughs and messes his hair. "Hi, weirdo."

I try to step back, but Lydia continues to nudge me forward. "And this," she announces, "is who I work for. This is Mrs.—"

"—Mary."

The niece turns from Paul and smiles at me as if we're old friends. "Mary," she says without an accent, holding my gaze until I have to look away. "That's a nice name."

"You look good," Lydia interrupts, pushing back the niece's short, wavy hair. "I like this." She kisses her on both cheeks, hugs her tightly, then kisses both cheeks again.

"*Preciosa*," she coos in a soft voice I've never heard her use with her son. "*Preciosa*."

There is a polite silence as Lydia helps Paul out of his jacket and carefully straightens his shirt. "We put your purse here," she says to me, patting a small table near the door. "Luz doesn't want it coming in the house." She glances over her shoulder at her niece. "You tell her."

"What she means is you should just bring in your car keys for the reading. Your ID has voices, and they interrupt. Like a bunch of people talking at the same time."

Both Lydia and the niece pause as if they expect an empathetic response from me, but I have nothing to add. I do not believe wallets have voices.

Restless, Paul brushes past us into the living room and begins roaming the edges, touching objects and pictures, taking inventory. He cups his radio against his stomach and whispers to himself over the muffled sound.

"Make sure her cell is off," the niece says, following him to the window. "And no shoes."

Lydia nods at her and reaches for my purse. "It's okay, Mrs. Lady," she says, "I help you."

After she takes my jacket and car keys, Lydia points me toward a card table set up in front of a sliding glass door. The main room is small and overdecorated with mismatched things: porcelain dancing ladies, stuffed animals, a bouquet of dried roses clipped to snapshots from a prom. When I am seated, the niece leaves Paul and comes over to the table. She checks to make sure I am comfortable, then lights a candle and sits across from me, all the while watching my movements in her periphery, careful to observe how I sit, what I touch.

"Write your first name at the top of the page, okay?" she says, sliding a memo pad across the table. "I tell people to take notes and use as much paper as they want."

She hands me a pen and nods at Lydia, who takes Paul's elbow and starts leading him toward the kitchen.

"I'm gonna go now, Mrs. Lady," Lydia says. "My niece likes to work alone. You sure you're all right?"

I look at my watch and think of the Realtors, of the racket my daughter's dog will make as the people step over the threshold into the dark house. "Of course I'm all right," I say, but as I pick up the pen to write my name, I can feel the niece's eyes watching me.

When we came into the house from Palm Springs, my husband requested time with the body. He went out onto the deck, and everybody else came in. I went toward her room. The door was open, and I remember digging through the dresser. There were clothes all over. Socks. I pulled her books down and people came in, trying to stop me. Then there was a sound, and I saw Paul in the far corner, hunched over the radio.

"Hi, Mary," he said.

After Lydia and Paul disappear, the niece scoots in her chair and looks at her hands. In the kitchen, I hear the refrigerator door open and then Lydia's hushed voice explaining something to Paul. On the other side of the table, the niece pauses, then places her hands carefully in her lap. "My aunt—she loves you, you know. She feels terrible about what happened. She hopes you understand."

I smooth the notebook pages and meet her eyes as warmly as I can. "My husband and I don't want to upset Lydia. We just want her to stay."

The niece nods and bows her head. "Have you ever been to a channeler before?"

I shake my head. "I'm here as a favor to Lydia."

"Mm-hmm." She reaches for the notebook and covers my name with her hand. As soon as she touches the paper, she smiles, then all of a sudden laughs out loud as if somebody in the room just told her a joke. "That's nice," she says to a space above my left shoulder. "They like how you dress."

"Who?"

The niece looks surprised. "My spirits." She looks past me, then back again. "The first thing you should do is relax, Mary, okay? I know this seems weird and everything, but I don't speak in tongues and fly all over the place. I don't use crystals or magic. All people do is ask me questions, and I'm like a gossip between here and there. It's pretty straightforward, actually. People on the other side are just people, and all they want to do is help. Make sense?"

"Somewhat."

"Good." She picks up my car keys and runs her fingers over the lock button on the burglar alarm. She glances at the ceiling, then speaks as if to a child. "You need to calm down," she says. "Don't get so pushy." She laughs and turns to me. "They're excited, your guides. They're getting all amped up. Should I just let them talk to you?"

I close my eyes, and when I open them, the unwavering gaze is still there. "Whatever you think you need to do."

"Right." The niece sets down the car keys. "Okay, well, the first thing you should know is that your daughter came in with you today. She's here right now, actually. You want to talk to her?"

There is a sharp sensation in my chest, as if a fingernail is pressing at the tissue. *"Don't you dare."* As soon as the words are out, I regret them, but there is nothing I can do. I take a breath and try to stretch my legs under the cramped table without touching hers. "I'm sorry," I say, keeping my eyes off of her, "but if my daughter were here, she would know I'm skeptical of all this."

"Mm-hmm. What's her name?"

I cross my arms and press them hard against my ribs. "Sarah."

"Okay. Sarah. *Good.*" The niece looks calmly at the ceiling. "She's funny. She likes to be called by her name. Does it surprise you that Sarah is with you, Mary? She says she knows she can get moody sometimes, but it's a good day today. She wants to promise you that."

I close my eyes, and something hard forms in my stomach like a fist. Without thinking, I move for the car keys, but as I do, the niece reaches across and covers my hand.

"Don't be scared, okay?" she says, scanning my face. "Sarah sees you watching for her. She sees you, and she wants you to know it's all right. She understands your situation. It's all right not to feel sad." She leans forward a little, waiting for me to react. "Are you hearing me, Mary?" she asks, but I am not hearing.

Get your miserable hands off me, I want to say. How dare you. But neither my body nor my mind will move. I press my eyes closed, and the truth is there whether I want it to be or not. Lydia coming to me a year ago before it happened and showing me the razor blades she had found in my daughter's dresser. Me, taking those razor blades and calling Sarah's therapist. Me, telling Lydia not to worry. To let it be. That it wasn't any of her business.

"You'll always be her mother, and she'll always love you," the niece continues. "Do you know that? She wants you to know. What happened that day was not your fault."

Please stop, I try to say, but no words will come. I don't have the ability to defend myself.

When I walked into the house from Palm Springs, there were policemen on the deck and four paramedics. They were in a circle around my daughter's body, trying to lift it from the hot tub. She was slippery and heavy, and they couldn't get ahold of her. One of them draped an arm over his shoulder, and the head slid back. I looked away. Men in uniforms were speaking to me softly, attempting to touch my shoulder, my upper arm. *She cut the insides of her thighs,* they were saying. *She bled into the water.* It took twelve minutes to bleed to death. Twelve minutes for the whole thing to be done.

Outside, a car with a large engine squeals by, burning rubber. There is a smothered burst of salsa music and laughter as it passes. It sounds like something thrown down a hole.

When my daughter was twelve, she wrote me joke notes and put them in my office. She hid them inside the drawers, under the cushions of chairs. *By the time you get this,* one said, *I'll be dead.*

I told her not to do that. It was horrible, unprofessional. "What if a client found one?" I said to her. "What would we do then?"

I try to stand up, to tell Luz Maria we're finished, but when I move, my ribs collapse and I start to cry. The sound is awful at first. Choked and tight, like someone drowning. I press my hand over my mouth to stop it, but the stifled sound continues on and on until I realize Lydia is there beside me. Her hands are on my back as it rises and falls. She and Luz Maria are speaking over me in half-Spanish, maybe arguing, but the words don't matter. The more I weep, the more I can feel my daughter all around me, hovering in the air just beyond my reach. Her face is broken and she is trying to touch me. "Don't worry, Mommy," she is saying. "Today is good."

Behind me, the kitchen door opens and I hear the chatter of Paul's radio. "You go now," Lydia says, but I grab her hands before she can shoo her son away. "It's all right," I tell her. "Leave him," and the three of us turn to Paul, standing in a pool of sunlight that holds him like a breath. He is radiant in the cluttered room, swaying in the bright doorway with his hands around the radio, his mouth moving faster than the words.

SEASHELL

Willie Green I met in Group down in Seaside. He sat across from me in a camouflage rain poncho that rustled so loud during opening prayers that Victoria had to ask him to please take it off if he wouldn't mind, and make himself comfortable.

"No problemo," Willie said to her. "You got it," and then he folded it up into a tight triangle shape that made me think he'd slept outside a lot.

In Circle, he introduced himself to everybody as "a forty-seven-year-old dreamer in a world without dreams" when we went around with greetings, which made me totally embarrassed for him at first. Then we all had to go around the circle again and name a fantasy animal to describe ourselves. I looked at the carpet and said "eyelash viper" when it was my turn, and Willie said he was a South American tapir, which was okay, except after Victoria was finished with the exercise, he raised his hand and requested to change his animal.

"I'm sorry," Victoria told him. "But I really want people to

138

try and stick with whatever came into their heads first, just for an experiment in self-trust."

Besides Pop and Didi and the kids, Victoria is just about the nicest person I have ever known. On the first night I came to Group holding on to Didi's elbow, she came right up to us and pulled me into her arms without even stopping to think about it.

"We'll take care of her, Mrs. Storms," she said to Didi, squeezing me tight. "This tiny little thing."

"We're very concerned about our granddaughter-in-law," Didi said. "This is Lonnie Olivia."

Then Victoria put a warm brown hand on each of my cheeks and stepped back so that she could take a look at me. I couldn't meet her eyes at first, but she lifted my chin up even with hers.

"Lonnie Olivia," she said, smiling down into my face as if it was a pleasure just to say my name. "Are you ready to forgive yourself, girl?"

The Coping-Forward Group meets in the basement of the Lamb of God Church on Tanana Street two blocks off the boardwalk. It's close enough to the beach that we can hear the ocean when the blowers are turned off, and sometimes in winter when the tide is up, the water sounds so close I imagine it tickling the foundations of the Lamb building or, in a bigger storm, slamming up against the double glass doors all black and frothy. Victoria always makes sure that new people understand we are nondenominational, but she is a Unitarian from Hartford, Connecticut. Sometimes we call ourselves the sheep and Victoria the shepherdess, but we don't say those kinds of things to her face.

When we aren't in these conference rooms, the Lamb needs them for Sunday school classes, so we have to use the mini-chairs that are for kids. I'm pretty small-boned myself, but all the men look like giants in the chairs, especially Robert Paradise, who is Hawaiian and weighs over three hundred pounds. Robert has to have Victoria bring in a special folding chair from home that she says belongs to her life partner, Yvonne, which always makes Pierre Aziz roll his eyes up into his head because he says people from his culture do not go in for those kinds of sleeping arrangements.

During coffee break, Willie Green wandered around the edges of the room for a while, and then he came over to where I was sitting under the yarn God's Eye altar and gave me a "cheers" with his Styrofoam cup. Up close he smelled like Pop, all cigarettes and sweat, and there were stiff gray hairs poking out of his goatee.

"Nice animal, by the way," he told me, and when our two cups brushed together, they kind of squeaked. "So," he said, waving his hand around the room like he was showing it to me. "Lonnie, isn't it?"

I told him it was.

"Thought so," he said, and when he talked his face looked odd, I noticed, like somebody took an old man's skin and stretched it over somebody who was still a lot younger underneath. There were deep crow's feet around his eyes, and long lines in the middle of each cheek where the dimples had set into the skin like scars left over from too much happiness.

"I'm curious, Lonnie," he said. "Where do you originate from?"

"Sorry, I need to go to the bathroom right now," I said to Willie Green, even though it wasn't true.

The rest of Group we had to go around the circle and tell the worst thing that ever happened to someone we loved because of our behavior. I opened my locket with Doc's commencement picture inside it and held it up for everyone to see while I talked about what I did, and I noticed that the whole time I was speaking about black ice on the road at Arch Cape and the swerving roll I took there on my twenty-second birthday in Pop's LeMans, Willie Green was staring at my ankles and knees, and the space on the carpet right in front of my boot tips.

"Anybody else have anything to add?" Victoria asked, after everybody took their turn except for Willie Green. "The floor's open."

"That means she wants you to talk, Dreamweaver," Pierre Aziz shot out during the long silence before Victoria could shush him, but all Willie Green would admit was that he was more a victim of our government's foreign policy than anything else.

After Group, Victoria gives some of us who don't have cars a ride home in her orange Vanagon. Usually, it's me, Robert Paradise, Pierre Aziz, and Stan Schick whenever his girlfriend is out of town. Except that night, while we were waiting in the Lamb lobby for Victoria to go to the bathroom, Willie stayed there with us, pacing back and forth at the bottom of the stairs in front of the doors. Outside it was pouring, and stormdrops smacked the glass like plastic tacks.

Willie Green wasn't saying anything, just looking out into the dark, empty parking lot like he was waiting for the weather to stop, but I could tell it was making Pierre Aziz very hyper him being there, because Pierre kept bending each of his fingers backward one at a time to pop his knuckles, and the toothpick he had in his mouth was swishing back and forth like a cat's tail. I knew he was trying to get me to look at him, but I pretended to be busy, flipping through the hanging copy of "In Jesus' Palm" on the activity board until finally he came over and tried to grab my arm.

"Stroke off," I said, but Pierre had already slid down the banister to the landing.

"Hey, Kawasaki man," he said in a loud voice aimed at the back of Willie Green's head. "Thought I saw you come on a bike."

Willie Green turned from the door and looked up at Pierre very calmly, as if he was a regular person. "Don't think I can get it started, buddy."

"Well, Homes," Pierre said, "why don't you let me try and look at it before we have to go?"

Willie smiled up at Robert Paradise and me. "Bike's old," he said, winking at us. "I don't think so."

"Well I do." Pierre took the toothpick out of his mouth and pointed it down the stairs at Willie Green. "You don't think I know bikes, Mr. Peppermint? I know fucking bikes."

Willie Green held up his hands as if Pierre Aziz might be trying to mug him with a squirt gun. "Sure thing, Boss," he said, trying to keep a straight face. "Let's step outside."

"You got it." Pierre sauntered past Willie and kicked the doors open with his boot heel. "After you," he said, sticking his hand out into the rain.

Then, after the doors slammed shut, it was just me and Robert Paradise and the thick, wheezy sound of his breathing until Victoria came back from the bathroom wearing a new plummy-colored lipstick that I'd never seen on her. I told her it looked pretty against her skin, and she squeezed my arm twice for a thank-you.

"Where's Pierre, though?" she asked.

I opened my mouth to tell her, except Robert Paradise cut in and started chattering away about how he couldn't believe that he, Robert Emmanuel Paradise, was actually in Group with somebody like Willie Green, who was in V. Nam with his uncles and dad. While he was talking, Victoria switched her long purse strap from one arm to the other. She smiled and nodded at Robert Paradise through the whole thing in that extra-patient way she has, because Robert had a head injury in grade school that makes him say and do weird things, like memorize all the names of the lakes from Washington to Alaska. Sometimes after Group he'll recite them if we ask him to, Oswego, Horseshoe,

Round, Cowichan, and like that, except he goes ballistic whenever Pierre Aziz tells him to do rivers or creeks.

Victoria waited for Robert to finish every word before she tucked her palms around his and my elbows. "Let's make a run for it, gang," she said. "Our boy is around here somewhere."

Outside, Willie and Pierre were standing next to the Vanagon in a pool of misty blue light from the streetlamp. Willie had the hood of his poncho up, but Pierre didn't have an umbrella or anything and his spiky black bangs were plastered to his head. The motorcycle was a few spaces away, leaning on its kickstand next to the Lamb of God Dumpster.

Victoria dead-bolted the entrance doors and linked elbows with Robert and me. "Ok, you two," she said. "Prepare to get soaked."

"I can't prepare," Robert Paradise said, which made Victoria laugh and take a deep breath.

"Come on," she said, pulling us into it, and as soon as we were out from under the awning, she gave a high girly scream. "Go," she said. "Run," and her acting a little crazy and alive like that made Robert start stomping on all the puddles flat-footed, trying to splash us on purpose.

"Get me, get me," Victoria dared him. "Just try."

At first the rain felt stinging cold, but as I ran, holding on to Victoria's arm, it started to feel plush and warmer, so I closed my eyes and opened my mouth, letting it splot down on my tongue.

"Lift your faces to it," Victoria said to us. "It's beautiful. Go on," and as I felt the drops reach down inside the collar of my jacket like grabbing fingers, I was so full of my good feelings for Victoria right then that halfway across the Lamb parking lot, I jumped up on her back, whooping loud, and she gave me a piggyback ride the whole rest of the way. While I was up on her, with my arms and knees around her neck and waist, I forgot all about myself for a minute, forgot who or where I even was, and

I pretended she was Doc carrying me, and as I pressed my face into the back of her beaded cornrow braids, her perfumey smell turned smoky, like his, and I could feel my whole body going away.

When we got over to the car, we were all out of breath, and Robert Paradise's T-shirt had climbed halfway up the soft overhang of his belly.

"Here we are," Victoria sang out to Willie Green.

"Here you are," he said, glancing up at me as I slid down off Victoria's back. "And I've got a little problem with my ride. Can I catch one from you?"

"Fine by me," Victoria said, as she dug through her big purse for the keys.

Robert pulled his shirt down over his stomach and asked Willie did they find out what was wrong with the bike.

"Better check with your buddy," Willie said, cocking his head at Pierre, but when Robert turned to ask him, Pierre was already holding up his middle finger at an angle out of Victoria's sight.

When we ride with Victoria, she has us rotate riding shotgun so nobody feels resentful or thinks there is favoritism. That week it was Pierre's turn to sit in front, so I slid into the middle seat after Willie Green, and Robert Paradise scrunched into the way back. The windows were all fogged, so as soon as Robert Paradise got settled, he put his finger up to the glass and started in with his initials in cursive. R.E.P. P.E.R. P.R.E. Victoria has asked him before not to do it, but that night, while the engine was warming up, she turned on the overhead light instead, and got busy trying to find something in her purse.

"I'm sorry, you guys," she said, "but if I lost this grocery list, Yvonne is going to have a conniption."

"Uh-oh," Pierre said, reaching over to turn on the heat full blast. "We don't want that."

"No," Victoria said, grimacing into her purse. "We don't."

In the way back, Robert Paradise drew hearts around his initials on the glass, and through the spirals and curves I could see the pointed spire on top of the Lamb of God, glowing like a yellow icicle.

In the middle seat, Willie Green's poncho looked like a wrinkled lily pad between us. He didn't look at me ever, but when the hot air made my teeth start to chatter, he reached over and covered my knees and thighs with it so that both our legs were under its green cocoon. His breathing was light and quiet, but sometimes, when he inhaled deeper, the air would catch for a second in the back of his throat, and that jag made my heart speed up a little, thinking how I was sitting next to somebody who might have killed people on purpose in a war instead of just by accident like some of us, somebody who was only fifteen years younger than Pop.

"Oh, to hell," Victoria said after she had emptied her whole purse and still couldn't find the list. "We gotta get out of here." She put the Vanagon in gear and looked into the rearview mirror at Willie. "We go Haystack, Nickel, Maynard, and I end up in Tolovana Park. Where can I drop you?"

Willie looked into Victoria's eyes in the mirror. "By the last one," he said.

"Tolovana?"

"Ecola Cottages, actually. Staying with a friend."

"You got it, Sir," Victoria said, yanking the Vanagon into a tight U-turn. "Hold on."

Instead of heading toward Pierre Aziz's mother's apartment house, Victoria sped us into the Mariner Market parking lot and pulled up next to the pay phone outside the doors.

"I need to call Yvonne for the shopping list," she said. "It'll just take me a minute to pick some things up." She turned off the ignition, and the wipers died midwindshield. Pierre handed her the purse, and after she hopped out, she stuck her head back in the open door. "Anyone who wants to can come in," she said. "But we've got to hustle."

"That's me," Pierre said, lifting the collar of his jacket up over his head. He bolted out the passenger door and slid open the side of the Vanagon. "Let's go, Paradise. You can front me some smokes."

"Okay," Robert said, and when he had both tennis shoes on the pavement, Pierre pulled Robert's T-shirt down for him and lifted his belt buckle up to meet it. When they were done, they both looked in at me, waiting, and after a minute Pierre's eyes moved to the poncho covering my legs.

"Come on, Lonnie," Pierre ordered, careful not to make eye contact with Willie Green. "She said hustle up. Let's go."

Except before I could follow, Willie Green slid his hand under my knee and cupped it there. He did it without disturbing the poncho, either, so quiet and stealthy that I couldn't move it or my leg without Pierre seeing.

"Come, Lonnie," Robert Paradise said, but as soon as he spoke Willie Green's fingers reached all the way around the top of my calf and squeezed so much warm blue electricity up my leg that the white window lights of the Mariner Market dribbled away, its butcher-paper signs advertising thin spaghetti noodles and rib eye roast, and all I could imagine as I bit down on my tongue was Willie Green in black soldier's paint, crawling on his stomach in the night along the jungle ground.

"I'm waiting, I think," I said to Pierre Aziz. "For Victoria."

Pierre looked at Victoria's back hunched over the receiver, still talking to Yvonne, then turned back to me as if he couldn't believe his ears. "Okay, wait for her then, Lonnie," he said. "Whatever." Then he crooked his elbow around Robert Paradise's neck and led him away like a big bear before I could say anything else.

Out the side door of the Vanagon, I could see Victoria hang

up the pay phone and head for the entrance to the Mariner Market. As she passed by, I peeked at Willie Green sideways, but he was staring straight ahead as if he wasn't even sitting there next to me, as if his hand was not anywhere near my leg.

After Victoria disappeared from our sight, I counted to sixty, then looked down at Willie Green's covered-up hand. "Ecola Cottages are nice," I said, trying hard not to whisper. "They're by where I live."

"Yeah, I've seen you over there," said Willie Green. "On Maynard Court. You're in the house with the old people. The one with all the whirligigs and the flag."

I looked over at him, and Willie Green smiled.

"Don't worry," he said. "I'm not spying. You're on the front porch all the time. Watching those things spin."

He rested his cheek against the cold window and the grip he had on my leg tightened. "What do you call those handsome little kids of yours?"

"I don't know if you know this," I said, "but Victoria has a rule. Nobody in Coping-Forward can see each other or anything. If any people see each other and Victoria catches them—"

"Hey, guess what?" Willie Green said. "I want to show you something. Watch." He closed his eyes and turned to me, and his face looked serene right then, like my babies do when they are sleeping. "Do you know what I can see?" he asked. "I can see you, Lonnie. I'm seeing you now, and you know what you remind me of? Do you?" Willie Green didn't wait for an answer. He kept smiling to himself, and the place on the back of my knee where his hand was felt like a throbbing burn. "A seashell is all," he said. "Just a little seashell."

"I think I'm going," I said, yanking my leg away from the hand. "I'm going in with them right now." I imagined at first, as I scooted across the seat, that he might stop me, he might reach out and grab my wrist or come up close and breathe on me, but Willie Green didn't do any of that. He let me go.

I ran into the Mariner Market without looking back at the Vanagon, and burst through the electric doors, past the office plants and greeting card racks and straight to the Brach's candy bins by the registers where I started filling little brown bags with candy corn and Neapolitan chews for the kids. I had five bags full before Victoria, Pierre, and Robert came up behind me with the grocery cart.

"There you are," Victoria said, and when I whipped around, I dropped three of the bags and the colored candy fell all over the shiny floor around their feet like a broken piñata.

"Sorry," I said to them.

Pierre looked down at the mess and shrugged. "De nada," he said, and the three of them cracked up.

Victoria paid for the groceries while Robert and I picked up the Brach's. She carried her two shopping bags out to the Vanagon, one under each arm, and Pierre followed a few steps behind, carrying the twelve-pound turkey that Yvonne wanted her to cook for the equinox.

When we got back to the Vanagon, Victoria had it started up, lights on and wipers going. I let Robert climb in first, but when it was my turn to get in, Victoria and Pierre both stared at me before their eyes moved to the empty space on the middle seat.

"How about that, Lonnie?" said Pierre Aziz. "He's gone."

When I got home, Didi had set up Arnold John in his playpen next to Pop's chair and Liddie and Jeanine were on the floor, playing speedway with Doc's old Matchbox cars.

"Here comes Mama," Didi said as soon as I came in, but neither of them came to me. Instead, Jeanine stood up and trundled over to Pop's easy chair. She stood in front of him and held out a red Corvette. Pop took off his glasses and squinted into Jeanine's face. "Which one are you?" he asked.

"Jeanine," I said, and Pop nodded. Without his glasses on, his eyes looked filmy and gray. He took the car out of Jeanine's hand and held it up in front of her nose. "You're a crazy kid," he said. "You know that?"

"Look who's home now, Father," Didi said in a loud voice to Pop. Then she smiled up at me and asked me how was the meeting and how did I feel.

"It was nice," I said. "I'm fine." And then she followed me into the kitchen and helped me off with my jacket and sweater.

"Group could be canceled for a while, though," I said. "Victoria has a problem."

"Uh-oh," Didi said, lowering herself down into the breakfast nook across from me. "What is it?"

"Something with her feet," I said. "It could be serious."

"Well, that's a terrible worry," Didi said, shaking her head. "Bless her heart."

"I know," I said, without looking over at her, and my tongue felt like it would swell halfway out of my mouth from all the lies.

In the living room, Pop hacked a few times, ugly and wet. He pressed the adjust button on his easy chair, and the electric buzz of it sounded like a bee trapped in the curtains. "I'd like to get to those greyhounds tonight, Mother," he said. "Sooner or later."

It took forty-five minutes to get everybody fed, and while Didi was giving the girls their bath, I called Victoria to tell her I was coming down with something and might have to miss next week.

"You seemed fine earlier, Lonnie," she said. "Are you sure?"

"Maybe," I said, keeping my voice low, "except I've had walking pneumonia before," and after I told her a list of symptoms, and she told me to get off the phone right away and go rest, I asked her something else.

"Victoria?" I said, and she said, "Yes, Lonnie?" and I asked her what if I was ever to meet somebody who could want me out there. Somebody that I liked. "Not as much as Doc, though," I said quickly, clarifying. "Never as much as I loved Doc."

Victoria waited for me to go on. After a minute she switched ears, and I could hear her hair beads clicking against the receiver.

"But Doc is dead," I said into the phone, because I knew that's what she was thinking.

I was on a kitchen stool, and I pressed my forehead against Didi's cupboard. In the other room, I could see Arnold John on his knees in the playpen, listening to my voice, staring at me through the white mesh.

"What if I met someone new, though?" I said, "and I was to ask them to go somewhere with me. Where do you think I should ask them to go?"

"Where is somewhere you'd like to go with them, Lonnie?" she asked. "Let's imagine some places together."

"There's nowhere for me to go anymore in this town," I said. "Anywhere I'd go, I'm not supposed to be there."

"What about the boardwalk?"

I thought a minute. "But the boardwalk is a mile long," I said. "You mean just walk up and down on it with each other?"

"That's exactly what I mean, Lonnie," she said. "For starters, just go to the boardwalk together and walk up and down."

"But do you think I'm ready for something like that?" I whispered.

"Hang on a second, Lonnie," she said, and just then I heard Yvonne's voice in the background telling her something, and while I was sitting there waiting for Victoria to come back, I imagined her in her kitchen. I'd never seen it, but I was sure it smelled like her and was decorated all in her own taste, and I could picture Yvonne there, too, with her sleeves rolled up, pouring yellow macaroni into a big pot.

"I have to go now, Lonnie," Victoria said, coming back on

the line. "I'm sorry. Yvonne and I are dealing with something. But I think a walk will be fine."

"You do?" I said. "Can I ask you one more question?"

"Sure."

"I'm sorry," I said, "but if someone calls you a shell, do you think it's meant as a compliment? A seashell, I mean. From the beach."

Victoria paused. "Lonnie," she said, "I'm sorry, too, but I really have to put the phone down. Let me think about it for a while, okay? Feel better and I'll see you next week. Promise?"

"Yes," I told her, "I promise," and then it was the dial tone and Didi was calling for me to tuck the girls in. "We're ready for you now, Mama," she was saying, over Liddie's high squeal. "Here we go."

"Wait," I said, "I'll put them down. Let me do it," but I couldn't move from where I was sitting in their kitchen, looking at the wall above the bouquet of silk flowers, where Didi hung the sand dollars and Pop's Audubon calendar and the cedar crucifix Doc made for her in woodshop with the words burned black into the center— "God is Watching."

And right then, right before I went in to do final diaper check and kiss the kids and smell their clean hair, I clasped my hands and bowed my head, just like I had earlier on the way home from the Mariner Market in the Vanagon when I was sitting in Willie Green's warm, empty place, and just like I would the following Tuesday if I kept my promise, when everybody in Group would walk down the stairs into the sub-basement, and Victoria would turn the lights down on the dimmer switch before greetings and say the verse from Matthew about Jesus taking our infirmities and bearing all our diseases just like Isaiah said he would.

"Teacher," she would say, holding the closed Bible against her chest, "I will follow you wherever you go," and then she would gesture in our direction and we would all join hands like links in a chain.

"Why, Lord?" we would try to ask in unison, with everybody always out of sync, and Victoria would answer, "Because foxes have holes and birds have their nests, but the Son of Man has nowhere to lay his head. Is this true?"

"Yes, Lord," we would say. "Thy will be done."

And two hours later, after we got up from our tiny seats, she would drive us all home.

AFRICA

I f you're wondering what I'm doing in Junie Greenough's covered pickup on the shoulder of a public highway, with a cooler full of Viennese horse sperm locked in the back, well, that would be today's very good question.

The ejaculate of the male Lipizzan horse, I was told by the second-string vet who helped me load it into the truck this afternoon back at the North Yakima Reproductive Center, can stay fresh longer than the life span of our solar system, if the material is frozen and stored properly. Only if.

"And Junie has the perfect donor for it, too," the guy was polite enough to remind me, slamming the rear door with his foot after we'd loaded in about twenty fancy shipping containers of the stuff.

"You must be new," he said when I initialed the receipt.
Well.

It was the last definition Junie Greenough would have for me at this point, but I told him I was.

"Be sure and tell her hello," he said, patting the driver's

door hard a couple of times after I climbed back into the cab. Hard enough to let me know he'd definitely slept with her.

"Oh, I'll tell her," I said. But that was six hours ago. Before I got to the bridge that connects Clarkston, Washington, to Lewiston, Idaho. Before I saw the Snake River start to rush up under me in the dark, and all the most recent gas station coffee was proceeding to boil up the back of my throat so bad I had to swerve over to the side and let what felt like all my insides go. Doubled over like a drunk teenager on the shoulder of the entrance lane.

When I was done, I leaned back and let the front bumper of the truck hold me up. A car or two blistered by every few minutes or so in a blinding flash. I didn't even notice the colors of the one that finally slowed down. Just heard the boots on gravel.

"Anything I can help you with?" he said. "You broken down?"

"Jesus Christ," I felt like saying, "shoot me now." But right then I didn't have it in me. He was a very distinguished gentleman. One of those state troopers who seems born into a role of honor and authority. All I could think of was I didn't want him to see me cry.

"You're obstructing a roadway, my friend," he said. "Do you know that?"

"I'm sorry," I said. "I'll turn around."

"Not here you won't," he said. "Not next to a bridge." And out shot the gloved hand for license and registration.

"Junelle Greenough of Yakima," he said, running the pin flashlight over my face and hair. "What's your relationship to her?"

"I'm a friend," I told him before he went back to run it through the database. "A significant other." But lately that's become a little more complicated.

At first I was Junie Greenough's student, then one of her employees. For a short while, too, the father of her child. I

don't mention "lover," though, among these words because
Junie's real love in the world, her only real reason for living
(and she says everybody has one), is Africa. Not Africa the continent, either. Africa the breeding line. Africa the horse.

Africa's full name is Maestoso XII Africa. Maestoso after his
father; the roman numeral twelve for the keeping of records;
and Africa for his saintly mother, anointed by the Austro-
Hungarians for some special equine reason that probably died
with whoever made it up.

If you saw the stallion, Africa, in person or, actually, *in horse*,
you might not think he has bodily fluids that everybody wants
for ten and a half grand. I didn't think so at first, anyway, not
by the looks of him, but this is just something that, over time,
Junie Greenough showed me was different than how it looked.
One of the things.

Take the frozen cargo in this vehicle of hers, for instance.
From the outside, it looks like any other covered delivery truck,
basically, but to people who know about The Lipizzan Pedigree
Trust or belong to the Lipizzan Association of North America
(including Junie Greenough, as its vice president), it is considered the nearest thing to a sacred shrine.

The semen of Maestoso XII Africa that I am in possession
of at the present time is worth somewhere in the neighborhood
of $300,000. It isn't an exact math, of course, but if each pure-
blood Lipizzan mare that is inseminated with it drops a healthy
foal, there could, in reality, be twenty-four tiny Africas riding
shotgun in the back of the truck with me right now.

"You look like an abandoner," Junie said to me the first time
I had my arms around her. "Messes to pick up everywhere."

"Actually the opposite," I told her then. "I'm a stealer." But
I didn't mention anything to her about my son.

What Junelle Greenough of Yakima doesn't yet know and
what Trooper Neil P. Lofton of the Washington State Highway
Patrol is about to find out is that somewhere out there, on this

dark road, far past the Snake River below us and the outer beam of these borrowed headlights, is the state of New Mexico, where there are several red legal flags waving in my honor. There are court orders 5629776.8, 5629776.9, and 5629776.10 to be specific, and on the bottom of these papers lies the illegible signature of Sharon. Sharon the Difficult. Sharon the Gorgeous, the Limited, the Insane. And somewhere, floating above all that, there is the name of Terence, too. My son.

The addresses, social security numbers, and official documents belonging to these names, of Sharon, of Terence, I no longer carry with me. They are in the bristles of trees, the roots and shine of stars, the highway dividing line, and night.

Junelle Greenough, however, is different. I met Junie when she came to the Elder Work Center of Yakima last spring for her big demonstration. Before I left EWC to be her hired man, et al., I used to teach the older folks there carpentry and the basic use of tools.

I didn't pay much attention to the EWC activity board as a rule—the job was not something I planned on keeping—but after the intercom announcement, as we all walked, wheeled, and/or shuffled outside to the baseball diamond (some of the folks with EWC screwdrivers and hammers still clutched in their hands), and saw the horse trailer parked by the dugout, I knew we were in for something different to fill the time. I was hoping, too, by the pissy look of the clouds, that it wasn't going to be rain.

Apparently, someone from the parks department had gone out and stripped the bases off the diamond in advance, and there, standing next to the pitcher's mound in square black dressage blazer, silk top hat, and starched white britches, was Junie Greenough, surrounded by grass and soggy dandelions in the Toppenish Municipal Field.

Some lady in a dressy skirt and heels, probably the new

director of EWC from Walla Walla, who I'd heard about but had never met, was standing beside her. And next to them, on top of the dirt promontory where the Little League pitcher for the Yakima Egrets or the Benton County Prospectors ought to have been, was Maestoso XII Africa, or as I liked to call him, the Big #12, throwing his head up and chomping on his own tongue and teeth, like he couldn't get them to fit right in his mouth. He was wearing his snazzy Stuben saddle and double bridle with the D ring, the same things he'd worn when he won a national citation only a month before. That's what the frilled blue ribbon was hanging from his brow band, but I didn't have an inkling about any of that hoo-ha and whoop-de-do at the time. To me, he looked like an albino plow horse, frankly. Pinkish skin around the eyes, a Roman nose, and to be very honest with you, a lot of spearmint-colored drool.

After we sat down, Skirt-and-Heels stuck a pin mike on Junie's lapel and tiptoed away as Junie hoisted herself aboard.

"Testing," an eager-sounding voice said to us loudly, with not a small bit of reverb. "I'm Junie Greenough."

After that, she slid her boots into the stirrups, and on cue, #12 rose onto his thick hind legs, tucked his front ones under, and started hopping forward, showing off, in my opinion, the most giant cock and spotted balls probably anybody at that field had ever seen.

Later, Junie would tell me that the mega hard-on wasn't such an aberration—lots of the high-level moves the stallions do are based on their mating rituals—but at that point it just looked embarrassing to me and vaguely pornographic. Enough to freak me out in a certain way, and slightly turn me on.

"This is my friend Africa," Junie said with a lot of breath into the microphone. "And he'd like to show you the airs above the ground."

When we were a couple, Junie showed me all the acrobatics Africa was capable of. Levade, courbette, capriole. But that day at the baseball diamond, it didn't look like anything to me except the way things were supposed to be. Like animal powers inside your body you never knew you had, doing things so far into the future and beyond gravity, you can't even remember or begin to describe what they are.

When Africa dropped down on all fours, Junie rode him over to the chain-link fence in front of us and did something I'd never seen before, not that I knew anything about what first-class horses like that do, really, in the first place.

Back in Taos, where I grew up, there was a horse pastured in the field next door to us called Baxter, who was rumored to be an old sprinter from Albuquerque Downs. Christ only knew what weirdo up there owned him, but he basically paced around the inside of the barbed wire with his teeth bared, and kids threw apples at him from the side of the field like rocks, including me. That was basically the extent.

Africa was something different. The Man (I used to like to call him that, too) curled his massive neck like a seahorse, lifted a softball-sized kneecap to his chest, and pranced there in place over home plate better than any baton-twirling cheerleader from Dallas you've ever seen. Every muscle of his body did a shiver, roll, clench, and release, not moving forward an inch but exploding in every direction with all that held-in propulsion, so that he groaned and snorted and sweated, his muscles rocking with the effort, giving everything he had in him, all his instinct, his wild forward impulse, to stay planted where he was while Junie alternated with the spurs.

It was brutal to watch in a way, and also beautiful. The way of moving that belongs to all things alive, I guess, who have that kind of talent.

"This is *passage before a charge*," Junie announced into her lapel. "If I was Napoleon Bonaparte right now, I'd spear my Russian enemy through the heart and bleed him where he stood."

Well.

After the demonstration, I have to tell you the Toppenish Municipal Field was altered. I don't think anybody, especially me, could imagine that Little Leaguers should be allowed to play on it ever again. Even the steaming green pile Africa left near the edge of third base seemed like it ought to be left there, like some kind of monument.

Now, I'm not a complete wimp—I do have certain skills—but it was obvious to me from the beginning that I was never going to get anywhere close to achieving something like what that woman could do with that horse. But for the moment I sure as hell wanted to be near it. Horses galloping full speed ahead on circular tracks for jackpots never made me feel anything like that. Trapped inside but also free. I just wanted the whole thing to be over so I could talk to her.

"Hard to believe, isn't it?" Junie said into the microphone as Africa bent down on one spotless white knee and dropped his head, bowing to us. "All this majesty created for war on horseback. Each movement like a lethal ballet, designed to kill."

Junie looked out at us then, scanning our faces, and all the folks around me nodded in their folding chairs with complete conviction as if they (instead of being a group of the aged) were actually a local gathering of absolute authorities on lethal ballets.

"Africa thanks you," Junie said, vaulting down off his back with far more energy than she should have had, and every single person, including me, could not stop clapping.

"Let us all thank Mrs. Greenough," Boss Lady yelled from the sidelines, but over all the noise, you could barely even hear her.

When I went up to Junie's horse trailer behind the bleachers that first day and told her my name, she grabbed my wrist and started shaking it.

"I don't remember names," she said, yanking me back and

away from Africa tied to his hitch, and the feel of her black-gloved hand, squeezing, shot right up my arm.

"He's something," I said, nodding in Africa's direction, trying to keep the image of the bobbing penis out of my mind, and Junie nodded, too, her fingers still locked around my wrist. "Yes, he is."

Africa snorted a lot of unidentified material out his nose, and I watched her watching him. To be honest, neither of them looked quite as good separately as they had a minute ago together. Africa was a trifle swaybacked, I noticed, and the rider had three to five years on me, but you had to admit they both had a lot of verve.

"Look at him," Junie kept saying. "Isn't he incredible?"

She was out of breath and puffing. I thought it was from the supernatural part of her demonstration, but Junie's feverish respiration, I found out later, was always like that.

She let go of my wrist and fell back against Africa's shoulder, letting him support her as if the horse was some kind of feather bed. "I'm a fall–down–drunk alcoholic without a hope in the world," she said joyfully, turning to bury her face against his neck. "Because of him, I don't drink."

Behind me in the rearview, I can see Trooper Neil lit up in blue behind the windshield of his cruiser, busy taking notes. His hat is off, and I can see there's a depressed ring around the middle of his large head where the hat has smashed down the hair. For some reason, this imperfection makes the man seem vulnerable, and I want to shield him from the information he may be finding. The APB Junie could have out on this truck and its priceless fluid, for instance, or the history of my halfhearted exit from New Mexico.

Apparently, you see, moderately successful contract builders who once resided in the Four Corners area should not drive their preteen sons over the state line into Durango after ten p.m. to a Chuck E. Cheese pizza parlor while in the middle of a particularly bloody divorce settlement. Apparently, some women who have lived completely sheltered lives with those moderately successful contract builders up to that point (before they parted ways to become bug-eyed and despicable remarried medusas) would define that action to the authorities as "custodial interference," and have them assigned to humiliating community-service diversion programs, regardless of the fact that that particular Chuck E. Cheese stays open until midnight and has the added bonus of a bowling alley (a sport the son craves) that happens to be open 24 hours on the Colorado side.

I lower my head and bury my face in Junie's lamb's wool steering wheel cover. It is soft, of course, and well made. Top of the line, presumably, like everything else she is in possession of. Except me.

The first time I came to Junie Greenough's farm, it was for a riding lesson on her old quarter horse, Ron Johnson. The directions she gave were confusing, of course, but the EWC student I asked to give me a ride knew where to go, and when he pointed out the sign and turned in to her property I had him pull over for a minute just because of the smell. Not totally unpleasant, but still astringent and sharp. Enough to make your eyes water if you'd never experienced anything quite like it before: *Money*.

"You can let me out here, John," I said. "I'll walk." And like every other male I was to meet in the town (even ancient citizens like John Ricoulas who probably shouldn't even be driving), he told me to tell her hello.

Junie Greenough's farm was a beautiful twentyish-acre thing to behold. There was a solid western view of Mount Mattawa and the foothills lined up in the distance, with a nice glimpse of the Yakima Firing Range in between.

Junie had told my answering machine in advance I'd be riding Ron Johnson. She'd added lots of other suggestions, too, before the recorder cut her off. To have an energy snack first, to get plenty of sleep the night before—and I'd followed her instructions. I'd even done some calf stretches on the road before heading down to the barn.

The truth was, I'd galloped plenty of ratty trail horses around before that day, but once she had me in the covered arena and I was up on Ron Johnson, I couldn't really concentrate. Not with her there watching. I didn't like the prissy saddle without the horn all that much, for one thing, or frankly, Junie, who was standing in the center of the giant dirt oval in matching camel suede, barking her military commands.

"Bend, bend, bend!" was one of them. "Breathe!" another. But the seriously annoying one was "ContactContactContact!" She kept screaming that word until I had to yank Ron Johnson to a standstill.

"What?" she said, when I stopped in the middle of the figure eight pattern she had me shuffling through. "What's wrong?"

"Contact with what?" I said, using as much patience and enunciation in my voice as I could. "The reins?"

And she looked at me like I was certifiable. She let her shoulders go limp and her head loll. "No, no, no," she said. "What do you think the saddle is for? Contact with your *ass!*"

Well. I took a deep breath and ran my tongue over my teeth, retasting the granola bar I'd just finished on the way over there.

"I've ridden before, you know," I said, edging the heels of my boots into Ron Johnson's ribs and setting him into a lope. "See?"

"Everybody's wedged themselves on the back of a horse before and hacked around," Junie called out, as I cruised Ron by at what I thought was a pretty good–looking pace. "Barely any of them have ridden."

"Oh yeah?" I said, leaning forward like a fake jockey. "How's this?" And I swung my butt around in the air a little the next time I went by.

Junie smiled and let the whip drop into the dirt. She motioned for me to slow down and bring Ron Johnson to the center of the ring.

"Congratulations," she said brightly after I slid off and handed her the reins. When my weight hit the ground, little dust motes poofed up, and they floated around us in the sunlight like dying fireflies and stars. "This man has too much ego and is too healthy to ride in any capacity," Junie cooed to Ron Johnson while she kissed and nuzzled him. "A person needs to be a fucked-up shit bird to ride classical dressage, right, Ronnie? No soul whatsoever. Like me."

After we finished and I paid her the thirty dollars I owed, I asked her about her big house and property looming around us, how she afforded it, and Junie laughed. "It all belongs to the Australian," she said. "Africa. Everything. Better do me fast before he comes back."

To tell the truth, it wasn't actually that comfortable or romantic to climb inside someone in the middle of a riding arena with an old horse watching, but the idea of it was.

"Goddammit," Junie screamed, on top of me, at absolutely the most inappropriate time. "We should never have done this."

But I was able to ignore it, and after I came, and sat up, and caught my breath, I looked down at the outline of our bodies and noticed impressions of horse hooves all around us and little dried pieces of their dung.

"You know, I absolutely loved that," I heard Junie announce from somewhere that felt very far away. "Hope we made a child."

Then she got up and bolted across to the barn with her britches in her arms, absolutely naked, to go worm Africa. Maybe it didn't happen just like that (time was probably collapsing), but I do remember I lay on my back in that covered arena on Junie's ex-husband's farm for quite a while afterward in my boxer shorts, watching Ron Johnson wander around the arena with his saddle still on, and staring up at the cedar beams of the roof (it was very well made) thinking, Wow. I am lying on an ancient grave of war horses, being trod on by their ghosts.

After I brushed Junie's arena floor off my jeans, I went into the barn and found her in Africa's stall, topless in the jodhpurs, shooting a syringe of white paste down Africa's throat.

"Now, there's something you don't see every day," I said, buckling my belt.

"You should put a shirt on," she said without a trace of irony. "Naked men make him jealous."

"Oh, come on," I said. "You're shitting me."

"I'm not," she said, running her hand along the jawbone of Africa, who happened, by the way, to be looking at me. "And don't swear around him, either."

I took a couple of steps back and lit a cigarette, and you can imagine how that went over. What was I trying to do? Torch the barn now? Drag her right back down? *Enslave her to the drink?*

Okay, so she was excitable, obviously, and ridiculous at seduction, definitely a freak, but I have to admit I liked it. By the time I showed up to that arena, most of everything I ever held in my hands had drifted past and away from me like debris in deep-currented water. It was rare to find a woman like that. So I didn't argue with her. I stubbed out the cigarette in the aisle of the Australian's barn. I tossed on my shirt. Even tucked it in, too, all the while looking over at the stallion. This Africa. Giant double stall, fresh sawdust chips, a half-naked, possibly pregnant woman giving him medicine. The horse was turning out to be a fucking king.

"Here," Junie said. "Watch what he'll do." She made a kissing sound and Africa curled his neck around her shoulder like a swan. More baby noises followed, and the horse started to bob his head, rubbing his giant cheek against the front of her breasts, freckled lips and stiff white whiskers quivering. Tongue out to lick her palm, and again, like I mentioned the first day, lots of drool.

"Look how he loves his mama," Junie cooed, and I wasn't sure if this comment was meant to keep me there or make me disappear.

Anyway, I didn't stand around watching the two of them for long. It made me sad, frankly, in a strange way. Like I'd missed some kind of love bus. Especially when I wandered back to the arena and saw Ron Johnson standing in our spot, reaching down to snuffle at her bra.

Both of us were surprised when her beeper went off. Shrill as hell. Not all that different than an air-raid siren. Old Ron Johnson took off to the other end of the arena, and before I could get over there to find it in the pile of her things, Junie came bolting in, whooping.

"It's one of Africa's babies," she said, pulling on her shirt without the bra. "I said to call when the mare is within a half hour. Trust me, this foal will be God."

She whistled for Ron Johnson and met him at the gate, peeling off his saddle with one hand and his bridle with the other.

"Ronnie's fine in here for a while," Junie announced in her breathless way, tossing the tack onto the top rung like it didn't weigh a thing. "Let's go. You shouldn't miss this."

I told her I was more the waiting room kind, and Junie snorted as she pulled on her boots. "Don't be stupid," she said, unlocking the passenger door of her truck and shoving me in. "I just fucked you, so dating's over now. What are you gonna do anyway? Call a cab?"

Yes, I should have said. Definitely. Call me one and the fire department, too, while you're at it. Please. I'm burning. But I didn't. I went with her to watch that foal be born. Tiny and bloody and dead. Perfectly formed bones thin as pick-up sticks, curled in its numb blue sac.

"He doesn't lose them."

Junie said this to the vet and the stricken owners of the mother, and she said it again and again with total disbelief on the way home, slamming her palms against the steering wheel as she drove down the center line refusing to pick a lane.

"It wasn't just him, you know," I said. "Maybe there was a problem with her."

"Then Africa would have overcome it. Genetically he's perfect. I'll show you when we get home."

And she did. Standing in his cold stall, she gave me the rundown while Africa dozed, propping his giant white rear against the wall, steam from his nose wafting rafterward. It was all Latin to me. This and that kind of superior sinew. How the Australian bypassed all the Spanish Riding School rigamarole to get him here, how the motility of his breeding material made that of all the other stallions look like pond scum. But what I couldn't really get over was the way she ran her hands over him. Her palms all red and rough. It was eerie, really, how I always preferred to watch them together. How watching her hands on his skin made me remember what they felt like on me. Confident and expert, like when she was riding.

"You touch him now," Junie said, her voice more breath than words. "Touch him yourself. It'll give you something to aspire to." And when I stood at his side and slid my hand along his barrel, feeling his whole digestive system rumble under my fingertips, The Man opened his eyes and turned to look at me, really, for the first time. I could see my face distorted in one large sleepy pupil, and I have to admit his stare was kind, filled with an inordinate amount of grief. I could tell that, unlike Junie, he could admit he'd lost one this time, that his big family had had a bad night, and unlike her, it was something he accepted. Even understood.

"Tell him all your troubles," Junie said. "He'll listen."

"I don't talk to Mr. Ed" is what I told her. "That's your gig."

Junie nodded like this made perfect sense. "Okay," she said. "Tell me, then, and I'll tell him for you."

"Madam," I was about to say, "you're out of your mind." Until I saw the look on her face.

"You think I'm kidding," she said. "But I told him everything about the Australian. It was his idea for me to get a lawyer."

I looked over at Africa, who blinked back at me. "I don't really want to know," I said.

"Sterile first," Junie announced. "We both had ourselves checked. Then later he went impotent. You'd never know it to look at the Australian, but it's true."

Well. It wasn't exactly a topic I wanted to follow out, but I have to admit I was relieved.

"I'm neither of those," I said. "But you can tell the horse I have a lot of debt. Thirty-one grand," I said in the stallion's direction. "All owed to a crazy woman. I'm sure it doesn't sound like much to you."

I stood there for a while letting the discomfort spool out between us. "That job with the old people," I said finally, "it's not my goal in life."

I waited for Junie to say something, but nothing came out.

"It's complicated," I said. "Maybe I better go."

"Hey," Junie barked, marching over and taking ahold of the front of my jacket. "I don't remember saying you could leave."

And somehow, before I knew it, she had my clothes off again, unsaddling me in one movement like I was Ron Johnson.

"We're both terrible people, I think," she said, taking a pretty hard bite out of my neck. "But doesn't it feel better to get it off your chest?"

"Absolutely," I said, letting her push me down into a kneel in front of her. "A real load off. Do you think your horse can write me a check?"

"Not quite," Junie said, closing her eyes as I unzipped her. "But the Australian can."

By the time I hear Trooper Neil's car door slam and the tarmac starts to click under the approach of his boots, I'm more than ready to press on.

"Can I have you step outside the vehicle, please?" is the question I know he's going to ask me, so I decide to hop out and beat him to it.

"I know I'm in bad trouble, Officer," I tell the man, "but I can explain."

Trooper Neil nods, holding my gaze with the focus of a raptor. We're standing toe to toe outside the driver's door, a couple of phone books apart. Close enough for him to read my thoughts, but if I ran now, he would take me down like some kind of khaki cheetah.

"The lady and I had a disagreement," I say, pressing my hands into my back pockets. "The truck is on its way back."

"That so?" says Trooper Neil, glancing around me into the cab. "How long has it been since you spoke to Mrs. Greenough?"

"It was today," I assure him, "around twelve or so," but I neglect to mention that, over the course of the afternoon, she's paged me thirty-two times.

"That's a while ago," says Trooper Neil. "Must've been quite a tussle."

"Not really," I say, and for the life of me, I don't understand why the man is drawing out the Chinese water torture. It reminds me of Junie, frankly. Of her obsessiveness. Her inability to try and unwind. The antidepressants she swallows with juice out of brandy snifters. The hay and dried manure all over the house. Jock straps belonging to the Australian still lying around in drawers. And Africa's daily ablutions, of course. The alkali levels in his piss. The cream used to clean his foreskin. The Viennese gobbeldygook of his family tree. Horse names mixed with other horse names to equal even more complicated horse names. And all the while, no genetic mix of our own.

In the first six months that I was working for her, being her carpenter/Man Friday at the farm (living there too), Junie appeared in five touring shows, a state fair, and an international dressage exposition in Vancouver, B.C. The phone rang off the hook with mare owners on four continents trying to schedule dates with Africa, but still she and I hadn't made a baby, and Junie was worried, even though I told her over and over she was forty and it can take a long time. Not to mention she was dancing around on a horse all the time. In the air.

"Not on a *horse*," she said. "On Africa. And maybe the problem isn't me. Maybe it's you."

It was inevitable when she said such a thing that the day would come. I just didn't expect it to be under my nose. With the sawdust man, the one who delivered the shavings every six weeks on an enormous, rickety truck. I thought I'd go down to watch her give Africa his bath. Number three of the day, as I remember, because he had to be washed down from head to foot between every sweaty love session with every single girl. I expected him to be soaped up by then, but when I got there Africa was still in his stall. I saw Junie holding the water hose in one hand and the sawdust man in the other.

I swear it wouldn't have been so bad if she had just let me do what I was doing. Just walk away. But she didn't.

"Well, I should at least try, shouldn't I?" she blurted after me. Which dropped my jaw, of course, and made me turn around.

"Tom is an old friend," she continued. And as if that wasn't enough, "I'm ovulating."

Well.

Who hit who first is a little blurry for me at this point, but we all three were throwing punches in the end. Teary sawdust everywhere, too. I felt it in my mouth when I called her a cunt.

The agreement later was to try and be more patient. If there was a baby around, Junie said, maybe we could be better people, on our best behavior. Sawdust of quality from another company was easy to find.

The morning that finally rocked the San Andreas started out as fairly routine. Africa's feet were due for a clip before lunch, and Junie said she would ride early. Her period was over ten days late, and we were disciplined. At dawn, we had done what we needed to do to keep it from arriving.

As always, with a nice thermos of coffee, I sat on the top rung of the gate and watched her school Africa.

"Looks great," I said when they were done, but Junie wasn't happy.

"What are you, high?" she said, tossing me the whip and reins. "We looked like shit."

"Watch your mouth, honey," I said, cupping my hand against her ripe stomach, but she pushed me away.

"Don't bother looking," she said. "There's nothing in there." And then she pulled down her britches so I could see the stain.

After she made a production of slamming out of the place, I gave Africa a nice walk to cool off. She'd never entrusted him to me on my own before, so frankly I was honored. Our whole lives revolved around The Man's wants and needs. He was still breathing hard when we got back to his stall, so I gave him extra water. And a few of Ron Johnson's molasses treats. "You're a decent guy, Africa," I told him. "A fine citizen. Good boy."

I can remember him licking my palm after the first sweet. The feel of his warm, slobbery tongue sweeping up the insides of my fingers was fascinating to me. Like the wet insides of Junie. I'm embarrassed to say it, but it's true.

And while we were alone there, I felt so close to him at that moment, I took her advice. I told The Man the truth: That maybe I did take that son of mine to Durango with some ulterior motives. Maybe it didn't start out that way at first, but in the end, his breathtaking and ball-crushing mother was right. It wasn't just for the atmosphere or the recreation. Certainly not for the pizza.

"It's almost impossible to imagine my boy," I explained to Africa, "as he was on the night Sharon accused me of trying to steal him." There I was, after bowling not even one strike, walking hand in hand with skinny eleven-year-old Terence through the amusement gallery of leering mechanical mice at the Durango Chuck E. Cheese. Watching them making their music through the yellow-tinted glass, those rodent minstrels. Banging on their hollow drums. Blowing into flutes and other woodwind instruments. Long pipe-cleaner whiskers quivering.

"It's a mystery to me, Africa," I said as I fed him those hard brown cookies.

I fed him again and again and again.

Two hours later, when I went to go get him for the farrier and he was lying down in his stall groaning, the veins on his belly all distended like they were, I thought he'd hurt himself in the workout.

"He pulled something in his leg or groin maybe," I went back and told the farrier. "It looks pretty bad. He's lying down."

"Lying down?!" the guy said, with this look of horror. "Is he straining?" And after that all the sirens started going off. The buckets and tubes. And the vet's questions.

"How many biscuits did you feed him?"

"How long ago, exactly, and what was in them?"

"This is an elite stallion on a special diet, so be specific. When?"

"Oh, Jesus, please," Junie yelled at me as I stood there paralyzed outside his stall. Her face all jaundiced as she and the vet and two assistants from the veterinary college tried to cajole the 1,200 pounds of horse to his feet. "Help us, Baby, now, will you?" she screamed. "Please! Come on!"

And I did try. I got down on my knees with them and pushed and pulled, like rowing a sinking boat with no oars. At one point his neck was across my lap and I was holding his giant head in my arms. "Lift," the vet said. "Try and lift." And right then I felt the real weight of Africa's skull, pulling me down through the water like cement shoes.

"Let me stay," I begged Junie. "Please. I'll make it up to you." But there were breeding shipments to go out from Spokane airport, and Junie wouldn't hear of it. "You need to do this for Africa," she said. "It's his legacy. Go. Now."

"I'm worse than the Australian," I told her. "You have no idea. I fuck up everything."

But instead of agreeing with that as Sharon would have, instead of hitting or blaming or lashing out and calling me names, Junie Greenough did something frightening. Junie Greenough grabbed my body with a new kind of violence and hung on. "The fault is all mine, Baby," she said. "I should never have trusted you with him. He's so fragile. My most precious thing. It wasn't fair."

"Don't," I said, covering her mouth, but it was too late to stop.

"I need you so much," she said when I tried to back away. "You're my mate. We have to keep trying."

And she pressed the keys into my hand.

Ultimately, what I know about Junie and her past is very little. She said she started out riding bareback in a trashy town on the peninsula, and after that it was off to Europe, where her shoulders straightened up and her heels went down. In the end, I know more about Africa. I know he likes his breakfast by six and his rubdown by ten. I know he has a small malformation of his coffin bone that needs to be watched, even though I don't actually know what a coffin bone is. Africa loves Miracle Mud leg packs, bromegrass, and Scandinavian oats. He hates per-

fume, quick movements, mood swings, and if he likes you
enough, he will bite. And this, when you come right down to it,
was the thing Junie Greenough just could not stand. Because
whether I was swearing, cologned, naked, jerking around, or
late, no matter what I did, even though I might have killed him.
Maestoso XII Africa? He liked me.

"What are you charging me with tonight, Officer?" I finally
have to ask him, because my teeth are starting to chatter, and
Trooper Neil seems willing to stand out here, just the two of
us, until the moon goes down.

"Would you mind if I grab a jacket?" I ask, and this seems to
get things moving.

"Just stay right there, if you would, please," says Trooper
Neil, then he starts taking a slow, appraising walk around
Junie's truck. "Wasn't sure how to ticket you at first," he says,
tapping on the rear doors of the bed with his pen. "Maybe just
a parking violation, until I saw that prior in New Mexico. The
chances of us keeping you in custody for skipping out on a New
Mexico warrant are zero point zero, so I'll organize a tow for
the rig and skip the impound."

And while I'm standing there, unable to form words, he
reaches into the cab of Junie's truck and tosses me the jacket.
"Unless you murdered somebody down there, you'll be out in
an hour. And I don't think you murdered anybody, right?"

Well.

"Don't worry about it," he assures me after my pager
decides to go off again. "You'll be able to return that call at the
station." But I want to tell Trooper Neil that his trust in me is
arguable.

The truth is I don't want to hear whatever it is the unpreg-
nant sender from Yakima has to say to me. I'm not ready to find
out whether the white horse survived his colic and is still alive
or how many times she has to call before she starts to think that

what I'm carrying might have become stolen property. I especially don't know what to do with her love or forgiveness.

The back of Trooper Neil's car, however, is comfortable. In New Mexico, I was never actually arrested, it was a court summons, so I didn't have the opportunity to free-fall into such deep leather seats.

"What're you hauling, anyway?" he asks as we pull away from Junie's truck, and when I tell him it's equine sperm on the way to Lichtenstein, this gets a laugh.

"Don't tell me," he says. "It's for the girlfriend." And if it wasn't for the steel around my wrists at this point, Trooper Neil and I would probably go for a beer.

"Horse jizz," he adds when I nod. "No kidding?"

And I tell him I'm not.

"Junelle Greenough of Yakima," Trooper Neil muses as he navigates us through the night currents. "Tell me about her."

But I don't. Instead I tell him the story of someone I admire even more. Someone who females pay to make love to them. Females from all around the world. Just an hour with him, in fact, is all they need. They will meet him anywhere and give of their bodies violently. They will bite and kick. And they don't mind where they mingle with him, either. It can be in a circle of Yakima dirt or by proxy. As far away as the continent of Africa.

"It's like an ancient fable," I tell N. P. Lofton. Full of triumph and glory. The hero has more living progeny than he knows what to do with. Sons and daughters far and wide who will forever carry his name. And, like the love of his life, the great lady who cherishes him most of all, once said, he gives lesser men something to aspire to.

THE WHITE DOG

The white dog was almost sixteen and would die soon. Every day the woman practiced saying this to herself: My dog is old and I will lose her. Maybe as soon as today. My dog could die in her sleep. She could die while walking. She could drown in the swimming pool or have some sort of epileptic fit. My dog will die in Van Nuys, California, U.S.A., the woman thought, and what will I do with the body of my white dog?

The woman's former husband, who had grown up in a religion she'd never heard of until they were introduced at an after-hours club sometime in early 1989, believed that in order for the spirit of a human or animal to safely leave its body, the body needed to be buried no more than an hour from the place where it had expired.

Her former husband, whom she still considered her best friend, assured the woman that there were good burial options nearby. There was a cemetery in Burbank, for instance, where

Trigger was supposedly buried next to Lassie and Fat Cat and Benji and Rin Tin Tin.

Whenever her former husband talked about the white dog's interment at the famous pet cemetery, over the phone, at dinner, or once in a while when he stayed overnight and they ate together in the morning before he had to drive his new girlfriend to work, she would nod as if she agreed with him, but the thought remained: What would be done with the body of the white dog?

One morning the woman, who was a sculptor sometimes but mostly a welding teacher at Mid-Valley Vocational College, took her former husband's advice about consulting someone and had a pet psychic come over to the house.

The woman put a muffin and a scone out on the coffee table, but once she arrived, the psychic didn't reach for either one. Instead she spent a long time looking around the walls, ignoring the photographs that the woman considered beautiful and focusing on some of the metal and neon sculptures she had started constructing a long time ago, back in Seattle. The psychic kept touching these pieces, especially the stainless-steel cross, running her fingers over the deep gouges in the metal, tracing patterns.

"Those impressions are from bullets," the woman explained after they sat down on separate ends of the love seat, the white dog lying between their feet. "I braced the steel against a wall, then shot into it with live rounds."

The psychic didn't answer. She continued staring at the cross for a long time, then smiled down at the white dog.

"It depresses her, you know," she said to the woman. "She thinks all this worry is ridiculous. She likes living with you in retirement, and she's not planning on going anywhere for a long, long time."

The woman looked down at the white dog, and the white dog looked back at her with eyes that could be interpreted as infinitely patient or as impassively judgmental. "Okay," the woman said, "but when the time comes, would she like to be buried or cremated?"

"She doesn't want to talk about it," the psychic said, turning back to the sculpture of the cross. "She wants to know why you don't finish any new work."

The white dog slept twelve to sixteen hours a day. She had arthritis in her left shoulder and ankle, arthritis in her hips, cataracts in both eyes, bone spurs in her back, and a small lump under her right foreleg that was soft now but needed to be watched in case it hardened. She had trouble seeing and hearing. At night she circled the house for hours, her nails clicking the floors as she paced.

The only sense the white dog seemed to trust anymore was her nose. She followed her nose into walls and down stairs. She was losing her appetite and weight. When the woman fed her, the white dog stared at the shredded chicken breast, the diced prosciutto, the chunked and seasoned rib eye as if she didn't quite remember what it was.

"The food itself means very little to her," the psychic said when the white dog refused a piece of uneaten scone the woman was offering. "Only the ritual pleases her. Your hand, lowering it down."

When the white dog was young, so was the woman. They had been together for over fifteen years. The woman got the white dog from a friend of a friend in Seattle. At the time, she was living with a Japanese drummer named Koichi, and the white dog saw many like him come and go.

When Koichi came home at night, the white dog would climb onto the floor mattress with them while they made love, and chew on a lamb bone. The woman remembered looking into the white dog's feral eyes as Koichi came, and thinking: I love you more than anything in the world.

When the woman got the white dog, she was in no position to have a pet. She worked several jobs and left the white dog in her parked car with blankets if it was cold, and water if it was hot, for ten hours a day sometimes, because the apartment complex she lived in didn't officially allow pets. In the parking lot on her lunch hour, she would feed the white dog half of her sandwich, a Yoplait yogurt, or macadamia-nut cookies with white chocolate chips. She would walk the white dog around the block so the dog could go to the bathroom behind a tree or a trash can, then go back to work inside the Kingdome, where she sold tickets for famous bands and baseball games over the phone.

Her worst fear then was that the white dog, despite seeming to love her generously and without reserve, actually hated her and was slowly building a case to either bite her in the face or run away.

"It can only be here on the premises if you're here with it," the landlord had told the woman. "And only for six months."

"Does she still love me?" the woman asked, and the psychic took several seconds too long before answering the question.

"Mm-hmm."

On rainy weekends in Seattle, after it was semi-over with Koichi, the woman's new boyfriend, a local photographer who had done Koichi's album cover, took nude pictures of her with the white dog.

Once he rented an underwater camera and had them swim together in a public pool where the photographer was friendly with the lifeguard. It was cold in the water, but the woman and the white dog looked good in the negatives the photographer finally sent her after she broke up with him and got back together with Koichi. Their eight limbs entangled in the blue water, the white dog looking like a cloud.

"Did she hate me when I was young?" the woman asked the psychic. "Does she resent her life? Or feel trapped?"

When Koichi was working his landscaping job or had all-night band practice and the woman was alone, the white dog slept with her under the blankets on the floor mattress, curled with her spine against the woman's stomach and her nose wedged between the woman's breasts.

"You treat the dog like an object," either Koichi or the photographer told her. "You love the dog more than you love me."

Of course I do, the woman thought, but she didn't say it to either Koichi or the photographer. Instead she smoked her cigarette and ran her hand over her stomach, wondering why she wasn't getting her period.

Now, with the arthritis pain, the white dog preferred not to share the mattress with the woman anymore. The white dog slept on several large pads near the bed.

"She says you shouldn't make this about you," the psychic said after the woman gave up trying to feed the white dog the scone. "It's hard getting old. If she wants to wander around the garden all day, let her."

"Burying her in Burbank with the celebrity dogs is a risk," the woman said to the psychic. "I could leave California."

The psychic sighed. "None of those animals were kind," she said, looking down and blowing hot authoritative breath onto the lenses of her glasses. "Lassie was vicious to every child he ever worked with. It's well known in Hollywood. They couldn't get by with it today."

"I don't know if I believe that," the woman said, nearly laughing. "Not Lassie," but the sudden and chilly silence that filled the living room after she said it made her quiet.

When the psychic was gone, the woman let the white dog out into the back garden, then called her former husband and told him to come over and fix the sink.

"I must've injured my back somehow," she told him. "It's really hard to bend down."

"I'll be over," he said, and when she hung up the phone, the white dog was standing at her feet, staring up through milky cataracts into the center of the woman's lie, her lips parted in a dark yellow smile.

In Seattle, after Koichi lost his allowance and moved back to Tokyo, the woman and the white dog rode ferries to the border islands of Puget Sound. They sat alone on deck eating hot sandwiches, watching whales shoot up from underwater into the gray rain, then sink back down. "In the far, far distance," the woman explained to the white dog, "is the border of Alaska. Maybe, in a few months, we could move there."

But that never happened, because life moved them south instead.

At present, the driving distance between the woman's house and her former husband's apartment is about thirteen and a half minutes. One freeway exit. Two stop signs. When he lets himself in, she is lying on the couch in the living room with a heating pad, feet elevated.

"I can only stay a little while," he calls from the kitchen. "Andrine is in the car."

"Oh," she says, listening to the bang of the toolbox, the sound of him opening the refrigerator and riffling around for a beer. "Okay."

"I promise it isn't yours," the woman told Koichi in a letter she sent him in Kobe, where he was studying Japanese spiritualism as he always said he would. "I don't want you to worry. Pretty soon I'll probably be getting married."

"Congratulations to you both!" Koichi wrote back, using exclamation points at the end of every sentence. "Come visit!"

And underneath his signature, he wrote the Japanese characters for "white" and "dog."

"I'm late, you know," she told the photographer four days after Koichi left for Kobe, and soon he was coming over twice a week before it was time to terminate, taking pictures of the white dog lying across the woman's bare stomach.

"I want more of you than this," he said one night and lay down with both of them on the bed. "Come with me right now. I'll drive us to Vegas."

"What's Andrine like today?" she asks, readjusting her position on the couch so she can see into the kitchen, where her former husband is squatting underneath the sink, squinting into the dark tangle of interlocking pipes.

"Pissed. She wants us to sell this house."

"There's a flashlight down there if you want it."

He looks over at her and grins. The white dog is standing at his shoulder, tail swinging, her nose pressed against the sleeve of his T-shirt. "I think your back is fine," he says, pointing a wrench at the heating pad she's lying on. "Faker."

She laughs and gestures for him to bring her the beer he's holding. "Thank you," she says. "Now fix the fucking sink."

On her back in the abortion clinic on Capital Hill, before marrying the photographer, she imagined the soul leaving her body was a white dog.

"Poocho Blanco" was Koichi's title for her. "The fourteenth reincarnation of the Buddha of Compassion."

Koichi had other nicknames for the dog that she couldn't remember anymore. They were long and poetic-sounding and philosophical. All in Japanese.

A year after their honeymoon in Nevada, the woman and the photographer went to visit Koichi, who was living in a Shinto worship center on Hokkaido. Koichi's head was shaved, and he wore a stiff brown robe that reminded the woman of the rain tarps he used to throw over his amps and guitars in the back of his truck in Seattle to keep everything dry. By then, Koichi told them, he didn't miss his inheritance at all. The meditation was more powerful than any sex, relationship, or even music.

"What about love?" the woman asked, and Koichi got quiet.

"I'm pulling apart from all that," he said, "becoming free."

"He tiptoes everywhere now, like he's gay," the photographer whispered to the woman when Koichi left the room. "Remember how he used to clomp around?"

"I remember," the woman told him, thinking of how healthy Koichi finally seemed, how the little padded socks he wore made his feet look like lily pads.

After her former husband returns to the kitchen, the woman walks to the dining room window with the beer in her hand and looks out at Andrine's Swiss profile in the car. She is sitting in the passenger seat with her feet on the dashboard, reading a magazine. In the year and a half since her former husband went to Lucerne and brought back Andrine, the woman has never seen her standing up, only sitting down in waiting automobiles outside, like she is now.

"What's her actual height?" she calls toward the other room.

She walks to the door of the kitchen and looks down at him, on his back now, his arms reaching into the greasy framework above his head. Through the open door, she can see the white dog near the back fence, stiffly marching the perimeter. "I'm going out there and ask Andrine how tall she is."

His laugh is muffled under the sink. "You're not."

"I will. If she thinks this is her house to sell, why won't she ever come inside?"

"I don't know. Maybe because she's pregnant."

"Yeah, yeah." The woman watches the industry under the sink continue, metal loosening other metal, then tightening it again.

Out the kitchen window above him, she can see the bottom of Andrine's feet, crossed and resting on the side mirror of his truck. Sighing, she pulls the curtains closed and moves to the back porch overlooking the garden where the white dog is standing in the center of the grass, braced on trembling legs with her nose in the air, meditatively urinating.

"Stop it, NO!" she shouts out the back door, but the pale stream continues to pour down the white dog's legs. "Crouch down for that. BAD!" Her voice is ragged in her own ears, but it continues to rise, even though she knows the white dog is nearly deaf. The dog cannot hear, cannot help what she has done.

"Motherfuck," the woman says, racing into the living room for her shoes. "I can't do this." She grabs the roll of toilet paper on the coffee table, the packet of Wet Ones that she carries around the house with her now, too. "Somebody has to help me, goddammit! I can't take my eyes off her for one second. I don't know what to do!"

Before she can move or say another word, she feels her former husband behind her. The heat of his body, the familiar pressure of his arms. He rests his chin on her shoulder and it fits there, like a part in a machine.

"Baby, please," he says. "Stop."

"But that's preseizure behavior," she whispers into his shirt. "We need to watch for it all the time now. The vet said."

"I know what he said. I was there."

"Wait. Listen."

Outside, the faulty fan belt on his truck has started up, flap-banging. Soon Andrine will do what she does sometimes. Drive around the block for five to ten minutes, then come back and blow the horn.

The woman looks into the eyes of her former husband. She realizes that she forgot to tell him that she found Koichi a few days ago on the Internet. He is a drummer again. Living in a small commuter town outside Kyoto.

"I'm Married!" Koichi had written to her in the e-mail. "So Happy!"

And for some reason, he attached a jpeg of the old album cover. The one of her posing with the white dog and her rifle outside the old foundry in Ketchikan, ready to shoot bullets into whatever impenetrable surface she could find.

But she doesn't tell him. When he becomes the parent he's always wanted to be, and she some kind of weird, secret aunt, there will be time.

"Congratulations to you both," she says, but quietly. To herself.

In the kitchen, her former husband is filling a bucket. Within seconds he returns, takes the paper towels and Wet Ones from her hands.

"Let me do it," she says, "I need to," but he won't give any of the things back.

"You're lovely," he says. "If I had my stuff with me, I could take the perfect picture of you right now."

And they wait like that, just as they are, for the sound of Andrine, honking.

LAST SEEN

⁓

Five days before *Abraham Lincoln's first home football game against Ulysses S. Grant, senior Jennifer Langsam, captain of the girls' volleyball team and National Merit finalist, discovered a pair of soiled men's underwear briefs lying in the bottom of her locker. The briefs, stained with an unidentified clear substance, were of a powder-blue color and had been draped over Ms. Langsam's white athletic shoes in such a manner that foul play was immediately evident, not only to Ms. Langsam and every member of the team but also to Dr. Jean Churchill, girls' varsity volleyball coach and director of Abraham Lincoln's physical education programs.*

Dr. Churchill wrote down an official, if abbreviated, description of the incident on her clipboard as she stood beside the tearful and obviously shaken Ms. Langsam, who claimed that she would be unable to practice until both the shoes and the briefs had been placed in the trash receptacle and the locker "fucking boraxed by a janitor."

Dr. Churchill promptly excused the girl from the afternoon's practice and put a teammate (Ms. Melissa Bone) in charge of escorting her to the TriMet bus shelter located in front of the school at 2400 S.W. Kokanee Terrace.

According to Dr. Churchill, Ms. Bone returned to the gymnasium premises within ten minutes' time, and volleyball practice resumed, after which Ms. Langsam was last seen by football coaches John Churchill, Donald Radcliffe, James McCortle, and Brian Apple approximately twenty-five minutes later on the A. Lincoln racing track, running 880s in street clothes and bare feet.

Head Football Coach John Churchill: "When I saw Jenny running like that, I blew the whistle and told her to stop. You run on a basalt track without shoes on—it's going to shred your paws."

"Oh God, my baby. My chickie. God. Oh God!" —**Mrs. Ardiss Langsam, Mother**

Dr. Vera L. Rose, Principal: "As a community, an institution, a living, breathing body. We are doing everything. Everything we can."

"I've known Jenny since she was a tiny, tiny girl. She used to water my plants for me when Ken and I had the boys in hockey camp up at Vail. I used to tell her, 'Eat anything you want while we're away.' And she really would.

"Once we came home and all our Häagen-Dazs ice cream was completely gone, and she had put the empty cartons right back in the freezer. I never said anything about it to her. Maybe she thought we wouldn't notice." —**Mrs. Martha Kern, Neighbor**

"Do you think I'm not thinking about it? Of course I am! What do you *think* I'm thinking? What are you thinking about?" —**Mr. Russell Langsam, Father**

Can you tell us your name, please?
Brian Apple.
Is that your full name?
Yes, it is.
And what is your occupation, sir?
I'm a football coach.
Thank you. And can you tell us, please, what you saw on the afternoon of October 11?
I saw Jenny.
You mean Ms. Langsam?
Yes.
And where did you see her?
Well, first I saw her on the edge of the football field. Then I saw her on the track.
What was she doing on the track?
She was running on it. I guess you could call it running. I'm not sure.
And what were you doing when you saw Ms. Langsam earlier, on the field?
I was with the team and coaching staff, getting ready to practice. That means taking the footballs out of the billow bags and setting them down on the thirty. This is when I saw Jenny, standing by the north goalpost on the opposite end. The track runs in a ring around us, so that was about seventy yards from me.
And you say she was just standing there?
Yeah. [Pause] And I waved at her.
You waved?
Mm-hmm.
Just casually?
I guess.

Dr. Jean Churchill, Girls' Varsity Volleyball Coach:
"There are always going to be pranks at the high school level

involving condoms and underwear, and during the homecoming weeks, it's going to get particularly bad. Some years I've seen them [students] all but wallpapering the halls with Trojans and Black Cats.

"In the scheme of things, finding a pair of stained underwear in one's locker around here before one of the first home football games is relatively minuscule. I have no idea what it was about those blue briefs that set the girl off."

Interview w/ Apple, Coach Brian (Cont.):

So, in order to see her there and just wave casually, you must know Ms. Langsam fairly well, is that true?
Well, I'm married to her big sister, yeah, so I knew Jenny all along. When I dated my wife, and then later, when I married her, Jenny was in the wedding. She was the flower girl, supposed to throw the petals into the aisle, but she didn't end up throwing them. She just walked up to the front of the church, holding the straw basket, and there was a big sisterly argument at the reception about it, I can tell you.
How long have you been married to Ms. Langsam's older sister?
Too long. [Laughs]
And her name is?
Kelly. Kelly Ann.
And of the two, who would you say is better-looking?
Excuse me?

Mrs. Ardiss Langsam, Mother: "When Kelly married Brian, it was the happiest day of Jenny's life. I mean it. The poor thing was so overcome with excitement, she forgot to pick up her own grandmother and bring her to the church!

"Of course, Russell and I were not too thrilled with Kelly marrying somebody. Well . . . we know Brian is a wonderful coach and an ambitious person, but let's just say Jenny was aware that her father and I wanted her sister to go on to college."

Contents of Backpack Found in A.L.H.S. Classroom 230/Biology Lab:

1 Red Canvas Wallet w/ TriMet Bus Pass, 2 transfers still available
Oregon Driver's License, #LANGSA360CDK
Cash: $5.35
The Strange Effects of Faith, Volume 2, by Joanna Southcott (247 pgs. with highlights)
Past Finding Out: The Tragedy of Joanna Southcott and Her Successors, by G. R. Balleine, Macmillan, 1956 (151 pgs. with highlights)
1 Jumbo Pack Trident Sugarless Gum (Cinnamon), 3 sticks remaining
1 Mead Spiral Notebook, College-Lined, selected pages used (See Report)

Mead Notebook, Ms. Jennifer Langsam, pg. 28 (See Excerpts):

The next time I go out with Dean Schumacher, he will take me to Roxy Heart's and pay for the whole thing, which, by most standards, is a pretty cheap date.

I will have the Dungeness sandwich. He will have the Reuben à la Roxy. Then we will drive out to Sauvie's Island and crawl under somebody's barbed-wire fence. And we will walk out into somebody's cow pasture holding hands.

The sun will be going down, and I imagine we will walk in the direction of that setting light until a farmer shows up and starts shooting into the air. He will come toward us with a gun, the farmer, and Schu will drop down onto his stomach in the grass.

"Oh, come on," I'll whisper to him. "Don't be such a chicken. You're doing exactly what he wants."

Schu will not seem to care a bit about what I'm telling him, though. He won't get up no matter what I say, so I will just hang on to his hand and keep still and look into the fading color without even blinking, until the farmer is right up on us. He will be old and hillbilly and panting hard.

"You kids better get the hell off my property," he'll say, shoving the muzzle of the gun between Schu's shoulder blades. "Now."

"All my sister had to do at my wedding was walk up the aisle with her basket of marguerites and sprinkle the goddamn petals into the aisle. That was all there was to it." —**Kelly Ann Langsam-Apple, Sister**

From: *The Cardinal Times/* **Back-to-School Issue/Sports Roundup Insert,** *Abraham Lincoln—Slice of the Month:*

Jennifer Langsam: Girls' Varsity Volleyball—MOST VALUABLE PLAYER
Call Her: La Capitana
Favorite Color: Cardinal Red
Favorite Flavor: Pralines and Cream
Worst Enemy: The Other Team
Favorite Position: Down Ball—Strong Side Set
Favorite Move: The Tandem
Ultimate Weapon: Back Row Kill off Weak Side Set

Mead Notebook, Ms. Jennifer Langsam, pg. 7:

Her Dream, by J.L.
I was looking out the window into the backyard and I saw

a mother badger in the driveway with three babies riding on her back. They were tumbling around. Then I saw a lynx. And I noticed the mother badger seeing the lynx at the same time I was seeing it. I put my hand up to the window and knocked on it to warn the badger, but the mother badger didn't seem to mind. She left her babies in a pile and walked over to the lynx and the two of them were kind of communicating with each other for a while, except the lynx kept looking over the badger's shoulder at the babies the whole time and didn't appear to be listening to whatever the badger was telling it. The lynx had those spotted tufts of hair coming off the tips of its ears. It was very pretty, the lynx. Then the two of them seemed to come to some sort of agreement and the lynx walked over to the pile of baby badgers and picked one up by the neck and carried it away. I guess to go kill it. There wasn't any struggle. I figured the two of them must have come to some sort of agreement.

Head Coach John Churchill: "If I have one player this year who's going All-State, it's Dean Schumacher. He's taking it all the way. You can quote me on that."

Hallmark Greeting Card (Dated 3/78), Donated by Mrs. Ardiss Langsam, Mother:

Dear Jenny,

Happy, Happy Birthday to you!

You don't know very much about me, but I know lots and lots about you. For example, I know you are five years old today!

I am your aunt Molly and I live in Redding, California, with my own little girl who is just exactly your age. Her name is Heidi and God gave her to me on the very same day you were given to your mommy and daddy. March the 12th!

I got this card for you because it had a funny horse on it with black buttons for eyes and patches sewed onto its skin that look like stars. I hope I can send you a birthday card every year and that someday we can talk on the phone.

Love always—XOXO—From your aunt M.

P.S.: Sometimes I hold my little girl up to the mirror and we play a game. We pretend the little girl in the reflection is you looking back at us, and we talk to her as if she is right there in the room. We tell her everything that is happening to us, like what we ate that day and what we wore. Maybe sometime, Jenny, you can play along with us. Maybe the next time you look in the mirror, you can pretend that the little girl looking back at you is really my little girl. And when you talk to my little girl in the mirror, to Heidi, you can pretend that I am standing behind the two of you, just listening. Okay?

May I have your name, please?
Antonio Hobson.
Is that your full name?
That's me.
And what is your occupation, sir?
I have a doctorate in aeronautical science.
I see. Were you working at Abraham Lincoln High School as a custodian on the evening of October 11?
Yes, I was.
What happened to you on that particular evening?
Well, on that particular evening, I came to work my shift like I always do, and as I was waxing the Science Wing like I always do, I found footprints.
What kind of footprints?

Blood footprints.

I'm sorry, could you repeat yourself, please?

You heard me, man. I said blood footprints. Going up the stairs into the biology room first, then back out of that room past the second-floor windows and down to the trophy cases at the end of the hall. There were ninety-six of them altogether, and they were making a beeline—

Ninety-six. This is a definite count?

You think I'm not gonna get a definite count on blood footprints? [Pause] As I say, they looked to be about a ladies' eight, eight and a half, and let me tell you, they were fucking strange. They started right in the dead center of the first stair, and they were dark at first, real messy, so as they went along, you know, I expected them to fade. They should have faded. But they didn't, okay? They went straight up to those trophies and then—bang. They're gone. Like whoever left them had just . . . walked off, for Christ's sake. Into the atmosphere.

Ms. Melissa Bone, Classmate

"I know she wasn't pregnant. I'm 99.9 percent sure of it. If she was pregnant, she would have told me, because we did that kind of stuff for each other.

"When I had to go to the clinic in the summer, it was Jenny who came with me. Some of the girls they gave Valium to, but Jenny told me not to take it. She said, 'Don't let them give you that. I'll hold your hand.'

"Up above my head on the ceiling, there was a poster of a forest, pretty trees and flowers, with a stream running through it. I remember it had a very nice feeling, and I suppose they put it up there for that reason. So you can think about and appreciate all the good things in your life while they're doing the operation. I remember I wanted to look at that forest the whole time, but Jenny wouldn't let me.

"'You don't have to look up there, Missy,' she said. 'Look here. Into my eyes.'"

Interview w/ Apple, Coach Brian (Cont.):

Well, I never thought about it, but if I had to answer, I'd say Kelly Ann is definitely prettier. [Pause] But Jenny is more unique.
Unique how?
Just weirder-looking. I mean, she has the same features as Kelly, except everything that looks normal on Kelly's face is bigger on Jenny and set farther apart. So you don't know what to think when you look at Jenny, because she should be pretty, but technically, she's not. Let me try to explain. Jenny looks better in pictures and from a distance, and Kelly looks better next to you, in person, except Jenny has the better body because she's athletic, you know what I mean?
I think so. Are you and Kelly Ann Langsam living together in marriage at this time?
Well, sort of. What I mean is, I'm there sometimes. Off and on.
Where are you living when you aren't living there?
[Smiles]
Fair enough. So, Coach Apple, when you saw Ms. Langsam standing near the north goalpost, can you show me, please, exactly what you did?
You want to know how I waved?
Yes.
Just in the regular old way. Lifted my hand up.
What did she do when you lifted your hand up?
Nothing. She didn't do anything.

Mead Notebook, Ms. Jennifer Langsam, pg. 28 (Cont.):

I won't do anything, but Schu will let go of my hand. He will put both of his own hands into the air and start to cry, to blub-

ber, really, just like a little baby—the farmer and I won't understand a word he says.

Then he'll start crawling toward the car on his knees and get
cow pie all over his cords. And he won't get more than about
ten inches before the farmer turns the rifle on me.

"What do you have to say for yourself?" the farmer will ask
me, and I . . . I will lift up my shirt.

"I'll tell you where Brian's living. In the basement of the fucking high school is where." —**Kelly Ann Langsam-Apple,
Sister**

Mr. Russell Langsam, Father: "No, no. My sister, Molly, Jenny's
aunt, has been dead for years. Jenny's sister, Kelly Ann, knew her,
but Jenny never did. Absolutely not. That was before her time."

Interview w/ Hobson, Antonio (Cont.):

*So you mention the "footprints"— that they seemed to terminate in
front of the trophy cases on the second floor, is that true?*
No. No, these things didn't just "seem to terminate," okay?
They disappeared.
*And what might one find inside the trophy cases themselves? What
is on display there at this time?*
Well, the displays are changing about every five minutes, but
right now they've got the Cardinal Cavalcade going. That'll be
up until homecoming closes. After that, they'll start in with the
Winter Preview.
What is the Cardinal Cavalcade?
Just pictures, basically. Of all the athletes and all the coaches.
It's a display of every fall sport, so they hang the pictures in a
pyramid shape. The coaches up top and then all the kids, the
athletes, underneath.

And in its history has the Cardinal Cavalcade always intermingled the pictures of both male and female athletes in its display, as far as you know? [Pause] I find ninety-six blood footprints in the hallway of my building, and you want to know whether pictures in a high school trophy case are co-ed? Is that a serious question, man? Is that the best you can do?

I am attempting to conduct an investigation, Mr. Hobson.

Yeah? Well, it's *Dr.* Hobson to you, my friend—and you know what else? I've been staring at your face, okay, the whole time we've been talking here, and did you know, man? You don't have any eyes.

I have eyes, sir.

No, man. No. You have eye*balls.* Not eyes. It's a different thing.

From Contents of Backpack: *Past Finding Out: The Tragedy of Joanna Southcott and Her Successors,* **highlighted text, pg. 3:**

One day to Joanna, a young maid came weeping. She had dreamt she was walking alone through the forest at the edge of Caddy Fields where a yellow cat scratched her right breast.

"Never go walking in Caddy Fields," Joanna told the woman. But a few nights later, at the same spot, she was found there, murdered.

Michael Ale, Employee #T237, TriMet Bus Co.: "I saw this young lady at 4:17 P.M. I was driving the #62 route, and I make it a habit to always stop in front of the high school whether kids are waiting there or not.

"On this day I was a couple minutes behind, and she was sitting in the shelter all by herself when I pulled the bus over and opened the doors. She had a backpack on her lap with her hands folded over it, and nice clothes on. Definitely going up to Council Crest. From a distance she looked like an old woman, the way she was sitting there, but up close, in the face, she was only a kid. "'All right—on or off?' I say to her, and then I saw she was barefooted. 'Whoa, whoa, whoa,' I say. 'Got to have shoes to come on my bus.'

"'Oh no, it's okay, Mike,' she says to me, and we don't have to wear name tags at this company. TriMet drivers are all identified by the vehicle number, so I don't know where she's getting that. 'No, it's okay, Mike,' she says. 'You can go on without me.' This is what the young lady says."

Interview w/ Apple, Coach Brian (Cont.):

Do you think Ms. Langsam did not return the wave because she could be angry or upset with you for any reason?
Angry? [Pause] Why would she be angry with me?
You did mention earlier, Coach Apple, that you and your wife are experiencing, well—
Oh, you mean about Kelly. No. No, Jenny doesn't know anything about our problems. That's recent.
Are you sure?
Definitely. Since that flower fight at the wedding, the two of them are incommunicado, and I mean totally. [Laughs] In my opinion, it's silly, but as you can imagine, I stay the hell out of it. No. Jenny doesn't know a thing about what's going on with Kelly, and even if she did . . . Let's just say that I don't think it's me she'd be angry with.
But she did, for some reason, refuse to return your wave on the day she disappeared?
Well, I don't even know if she *saw* me, really. She just kept standing by the goalpost, kind of staring down the field and holding her backpack like it was a baby, sort of cradling it, in a way. So I went back to what I was doing, and when I looked up

again, she was running around the track with those arms—her arms out—just like they were airplane wings.

This is when you noticed she was also barefoot, correct?

Correct. And she was puffing her cheeks in and out as she ran, really hauling ass.

And where was the backpack at this time?

Oh. I'm pretty sure it was on her back.

You're pretty sure?

I think it was.

Thank you, Coach Apple. Thank you for coming down here today.

No problem.

Melissa Bone, Classmate

"The day before she disappeared, I remember Jenny wanted me to go with her to the Galleria. They were having a sale at Vinyl Village, and we were digging through a big box of discount Walkmans. They had them in a bunch of different colors, but she said she wanted a yellow one. She had to have that color, only that color, and of course there wasn't one, so we had to go through the whole stupid box.

"I didn't think it was that big a deal, but Jenny was really intense about finding a yellow one for some reason, she's like that about things sometimes. She'll get a thing in her head and she just won't give it up, it's like she *can't* almost, so we started taking them out one at a time, until I noticed Jenny had stopped and was staring into the video monitor up above our heads, you know, where it shows on a screen who's walking by outside on the mall. She was staring at it with her mouth open in kind of a goofy way.

"'What's your problem?' I said to her. 'What's the matter?'

"And she said, 'My aunt is here. My aunt Molly. I saw her walk by on the screen.'

"I said it was cool if she wanted to go say hi, but she didn't. She smiled at me and said she didn't need to, never mind. So we went back to looking through the box. But I thought it was weird and a little bit rude, you know, that she never went out there to see her aunt."

Dr. Vera L. Rose, Principal: "I am an educator, a facilitator, a highly educated woman. But first I am a mother. No one has to tell me about pain."

"I was never a fucking kangaroo. Never." —**Kelly Ann Langsam-Apple, Sister**

Mead Notebook, Ms. Jennifer Langsam, pg. 41:

In his book, *Past Finding Out: The Tragedy of Joanna Southcott and Her Successors,* Mr. G. R. Balleine says Mary Bateman did good business in Leeds as a wise woman, abortionist, and professional thief whose specialty was "screwing down." If you had an enemy, you brought Mary a picture of his likeness along with four screws and four guineas, and his power to hurt you vanished.

When trade was slack, she would invent people to screw down, a hussy scheming to seduce your husband or a rake with designs on your daughter.

When she heard about Joanna Southcott, Mr. Balleine said Mary saw new possibilities. She secured a seal and posed as a preacher and showed eggs inscribed CRIST IS COMING, which she said her hens were laying.

Team Interview #5: Vealbig, Troy, Defensive End, A.L.H.S.:

I've heard from some of your teammates that things can get pretty crazy around here at homecoming time. Is that true?

[Shakes head]

No?

[Pause] Maybe. Which ones told you that?

Son, it's not my job to name names. I'm just thinking that, well, you guys seem to be working pretty hard on the field right now.

Our team always works hard.

Exactly. So don't you think with all that hard practice that sometimes you guys might like to blow off a little steam?

What do you mean?

I mean do you think it's possible, considering how hard you're working, for stray underwear to switch places or even locker rooms from time to time, just as a joke?

Maybe my team doesn't think something like that would be very funny.

You're right. But maybe it wasn't meant to be funny. Maybe it was meant to be some sort of threat.

There are plenty of other people who use the basement around here besides us.

Can you be more specific?

Not really. Why don't you ask my coach?

Dean Schumacher, Classmate: "Day before yesterday I took her to Roxy Heart's, which is a really nice restaurant. She had the Dungeness sandwich. I had the Reuben à la Roxy, and then we decided to go up to the Museum of Science and Industry.

"Neither of us were there since we were little kids, so we looked at the beehive and the baby chickens in the incubator and the two-headed sheep and this pair of shrivelly black lungs they took out of a two-pack-a-day smoker that kind of shudder in and out, like they are really breathing.

"So we looked at all that stuff. And then Jenny wanted to go upstairs into the giant heart. It's about as high as a two-story building, and you can walk right through the center of it on a little rubber track.

"One side is the aorta, and the other side is the ventricles, and it's painted all purple and red. The veins wrap around it on the outside too, just like a real heart. Inside, it's musty and kind of smells like feet, and there is a recorded sound of the heart beating and then, out of all the loudspeakers, it tells you the story of the human heart in the human heart's own voice. Describing the path of blood through your body for you.

"And in one special part of it, on one wall way in the back, is a glass cabinet with a real heart in it. Actually, it's only a collie's heart, but they've got it hanging on this little piano wire, and they run electricity through the center of it every so often to make it beat. The whole thing is lit up with a cool yellow strobe light, too. That's where she really wanted to go. In that passage-way by the actual heart. That's where she wanted to do it."

Mead Notebook, Ms. Jennifer Langsam, pg. 10:

MY KILLSHOT by J.L.

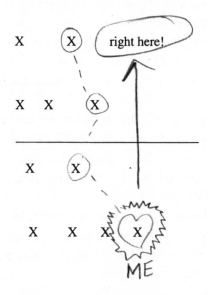

"There has never been any discord between my two daughters. Brian and Jenny were thick as thieves over sports, and Jenny absolutely worshipped her sister from day one. I mean it. In her eyes, Kelly Ann just walked on water. One Halloween, I remember. Kelly Ann was the mother kangaroo, and Jenny was the baby who rode in this giant pouch in the stomach of the costume. Isn't that darling? Both with big kangaroo ears. Somewhere I have a picture of that." —**Ardiss Langsam, Mother**

Freddie Mae Greer, Housekeeper: "I don't go near that child anymore. Not anywhere near. My Wednesdays since the school started, I don't ever have to see her. She ain't home. But my Fridays, whenever I run the vacuum now, she's following me, watching me in the kitchen between the railings on the banister.

"Friday before last, she comes downstairs, and what do you think she's wearing? She's wearing a big old wedding dress with the tennis shoes up under it, with that damn volleyball stuck up under her arm, stepping right across my wet floor, like she's just walking outside to the pool.

"'Child, please,' I say to her. 'Get out of that. You know you're not supposed to be in that.'

"And she says, 'It's my sister's. I can wear it anytime I want.'

"'Oh no, you ain't,' I told her. 'You ain't.'

"And she says, 'Call Kelly, then, Freddie. Ask her, why don't you?'

"Then she just goes rustling on by, out to the sliding door. So I finish up my floors and I go outside, too, and she's on the patio furniture now, just sitting by the water in her sister's dress, and she's a crazy-looking girl, Jenny. She ain't pretty and tame like her sister one bit.

"'Where did you get that anyway, it's your sister's,' I said, going over to her with the brush in my hand. 'I'm calling your sister. I'll tell her you're about to jump in that pool with all her clothes.'

"But she doesn't care, nothing.

"'Freddie,' she says. 'You know who I'm supposed to be?' And she's looking me in the eye, too, right through the veil.

"'No,' I say to her. 'Who're you?'

"And she says, 'I'm a voice.' Just like that."

Miss Eleanor Mayes, Forensics Instructor: "Jenny Langsam is fabulous. Bright, inquisitive, perfectionistic. Notice that I say 'is.' Several weeks ago, she came to me and told me she wanted to do her autumn interpretive project about someone named Joanna Southcott. Now, I had never heard of this person, but I told her it was absolutely fine. You don't know how many speeches about Colleen McCullough and Nancy Friday I have to sit through."

Vandalism on Volleyball #12 / Red Ink / Indelible:

I AM MY NAME

Mrs. Ardiss Langsam, Mother: "It was Jenny who took the call about Russell's sister. Now, this is just the reason I did not encourage my girls to ever touch telephones when they were little.

"We were having a get-together, and here comes Jenny out to find me in her nightgown.

"'It's a lady, Mom,' she says to me. 'From Little Chapel of the Bells. She has a body there, and she wants to know, does it belong to us?'

"Well, of course, I race to the telephone to find out what in heaven's name is going on, and I find out that this unspeakable woman from the funeral home—she has already taken the liberty of describing what Molly . . . what she did to herself . . . to my five-year-old daughter.

"Now, can you imagine what kind of a person would do

something like that? Would call someone's private home in the middle of the night and say such terrible, inappropriate things without even checking. And how could you not know you were talking to a child?"

Excerpt from Interview w/ Radcliffe, Coach Donald, pg. 2:

So, after you saw Coach John Churchill blow the whistle at Ms. Langsam, who was running on the track, what happened?
Well, she didn't stop right away. She did another 880 with her arms out like a bird and her neck held all the way back. It's just about impossible to run in that position for any length of time without snapping something, and when she was done, you could tell she was beat. She bent over and put her hands on her knees to cool out and she was in that position for quite a while, panting like that.
And what happened during that time, while she was "cooling out"?
How do you mean?
I mean did anyone go over to her?
No, well . . . not really. Number eighty-seven, Dean Schumacher, our wide receiver, he tried. He got a towel from the manager and asked if he could take it over to her, because apparently, they had a little thing together. I'd seen her hanging around with Schu before. I said fine, take her the towel, but Coach Apple told us to get back in line. He blew the whistle right then for the huddle, and I'm the low man on the totem pole around here. I didn't argue. We still had to whip Grant's ass in a couple of days.
What happened after that?
After that we practiced. We practiced, and I didn't think about it again, to be honest. I figured she just went home. But if I'd known, you know, what was going to happen, Jesus. I would have paid closer attention.

From Miss Eleanor Mayes, Forensics Instructor (Rec'd. 10/13—*Columbia Encyclopedia*, 3rd Edition, pg. 2,574, paraphrased):

Southcott, Joanna, 1750–1814. English religious visionary, uneducated, even illiterate. Spends earlier years in domestic service. Begins c. 1792 to claim gift of prophecy with "revelations" that attract many followers. Later, announces she will be mother of the coming Messiah as woman in Revelation 12. Dies of brain disease at 64, after time set for birth of "The Second Shiloh." After death, followers continue to study 60 or more tracts of her writing; sect never completely dies out.

Can you tell me your name again, please?
You remember my name.
And you are the custodian, is that right?
I work as a custodian, yes.
And you are seeking to amend your statement about the "blood" footprints, I take it?
No. No, those footprints were there. I just have something else to say.
All right.
The day before the girl disappeared, I found some other stuff that I didn't mention to you the last time we talked.
Really. What "stuff" was that?
A toaster oven. With an English muffin inside it. And a melted plastic fork.
I see. Where exactly did you find this "stuff," as you call it?
In a duct.
I beg your pardon?
I found them inside a heating duct that connects the two locker rooms down here. The boys and the girls.
I'm sorry. Let me get this straight. You found evidence in a heating

duct—inside a wall—and you didn't mention it to anybody until now? Why is that?

[Pause] I was scared.

Scared? Scared of what, may I ask?

The building.

You were scared of the building itself? I'm afraid I don't understand.

[Pause] Something's very wrong in this place, man. You should trust me on it.

What were you doing inside a heating duct in the first place, Dr. Hobson? Again, if you do not mind my asking?

I was listening.

Listening to what? What were you listening to?

Just listening, okay?

Kelly Ann Langsam-Apple, Sister: "Please. Our aunt Molly never had any daughter. She was a total freak. My sister and I heard from her when we were kids, but only because we had to. Our mother used to let her write to us behind my father's back. She was just a barrel full of monkeys, that Molly. If you like people on Haldol who try to carve off their own face."

Mrs. Sondra Stetson, Tenant, Raleighwood Apartments, #308:

"Considering they're newlyweds, they fight like absolute cats and dogs. Everyone in this complex is sick to death of it, and they only moved in three months ago. And let me tell you, we are just as glad he's only around here on the Wednesdays now when she's not at home. He's a real preening peacock, that one. I don't envy her one bit.

"A couple of mornings ago was the worst. He shows up at maybe ten, ten-thirty the night before, and we can hear bickering off and on all night long. Her voice is really up there this time, too. He's a cocksucker one minute, a filthy goddamn liar the next.

"Anyway, we've heard it all before from these two and tonight is par excellence. She's gonna find out who it is . . . and when she does . . . blah, blah, blah—and then there's all the crying and the making up. We get to hear every bit of *that* lovely business, too, and I mean *loud*.

"It goes back and forth like that until dawn, when the wife finally goes out onto the lanai in her bathrobe and starts throwing things over the railing. It sounds like bombs are dropping out there. By then I have to come out to investigate, and when I do, she's in the middle of heaving this toaster oven down into the parking lot, aiming for either the husband or his Mustang, I'm not sure which. And the most horrible, vicious sound is coming out of her as she's staggering around on the balcony with the cord of that toaster oven dragging along behind her. Like some kind of animal. I don't know any other way to describe it. The husband, he's in sweatpants and baseball hat and whistle, no shirt whatsoever, and he's standing down there trying to catch everything she's throwing—jockstraps, socks, you name it. Underwear in every color of the rainbow is flying around like ticker tape. It's a sight, I'm telling you, so early in the morning, because right behind them, these two, is the most beautiful sunrise I've ever seen on Scholls Ferry Road, just really phenomenal, all pink and gold and ripped crimson. I have to look at it for a minute, at the sun just tearing through the sky. I notice things like that, and it takes me a minute to come back to myself, you know, but I do.

"'Now, honey,' I say to her first, 'should I call someone?' And then, when she doesn't respond, I lean over the railing and call down to the husband, 'I think I should call someone.'

"But the husband, he only looks up at me and waves.

"'Oh, no, that's okay, Ms. Stetson,' he says to me, just as

peppy as you please. 'Go on back to bed now. We're almost done here. It's all right.'"

Handwritten Inscription from Title Page:
The Strange Effects of Faith, Vol. 2, by Joanna Southcott (247 pgs. with highlights):

> *Now she is barefooted.*
> *Resolute.*
> *Full of an unearthly conviction*
> *Because she knows.*
>
> *She is changing shape.*

Mr. Russell Langsam, Father: "My sister, Molly, was nothing but a liar."

Mrs. Ardiss Langsam, Mother: "When they announced their engagement, I have to tell you, I went into that kitchen and I lost it. I just . . . I don't know. But Jenny followed me in there. She was in her volleyball uniform, about to go to practice with those horrible, dingy kneepads on, and she shook me, really grabbed on to my shoulders and shook me, hard, until my teeth rattled in my head.

"'Kelly and I love Brian, Mom,' she said. 'So should you and so should Dad.'

"And she was just so fierce about it, I was embarrassed. Having Brian still standing out in the living room after what I had done to humiliate him on his engagement day. My God, I couldn't go back in there right away, so Jenny went in for me and asked Brian if he could drive her down to practice, so I'd have a chance to fix myself up a bit. She and I agreed it was a good idea to keep him out of the house for a while. It was dark by the time they got back, but by then Russell and Kelly had the champagne poured, and we were all going about our business like it was the best news in the world. Ultimately, because of Jenny. Because of how much she loved her sister. Because of . . . Oh God. I'm going to have to stop myself here."

Interview with Hobson, Antonio (Cont.):

So . . . what I think you're saying, Dr. Hobson, and correct me if I'm wrong, is that you consider the physical plant, the building itself, Lincoln High School, to be responsible for the disappearance of Jennifer Langsam? Is this true?
I never said it was the building. I said she was lifted.
Lifted. By "lifted" you mean kidnapped . . . you mean taken by someone?
No. I mean lifted. By a force. There's a whole hierarchy of them out there. Venerates, Dominations, Yazatas. Somebody must have wanted her.

"No body, no witnesses, no evidence, no nothing. So I guess that's an easy one, right? My sister was abducted by aliens."—**Kelly Ann Langsam-Apple, Sister**

Cynthia Blachley, Author, *EVANESCERE: Notes from the Files of the Missing,* **Houghton Mifflin, 1991:**

If one stands in front of the trophy cases on the second floor of Abraham Lincoln High School at the approximate spot at which these footprints in blood are reported to have disappeared, the subject sees one of two images. One either looks in and sees the pyramid of smiling athletes and their coaches. Or one looks past them, into the glass, and sees, as in a mirror, a sharper reflection of oneself.

I think the question we have to ask ourselves here is in regard to what was actually being witnessed. In other words, was the vanished simply looking in at some photographs, or was she contemplating something far deeper, in the reflection of her own face?

Mead Notebook, Ms. Jennifer Langsam, pg. 28 (Cont.):

"There's an angel in my stomach," I will say to him. "Why don't you try and shoot it out?"

And before the farmer can say anything, I will grab the muzzle of that rifle and pull it up against my belly button so he can feel the two pulses beating under it. Then I'll look at the farmer and he will look at me and all at once I'll feel such tenderness toward him, such a quiet gentleness, even though I know that if I wanted to, I could rip open his chest and eat out his heart in the space of one breath.

"Go ahead," I'll tell him. "Do it."

And right as he's about to pull the trigger, I will notice there are little clots of mud caught in his eyelashes.

Past Finding Out: The Tragedy of Joanna Southcott and Her Successors, highlighted text, pg. 12:

"I have heard my name called," Joanna said. "In an audible voice."

No one can understand how the visitation comes, how the words of the heavenly messengers, though perfectly formed, cannot be understood by a bodily ear.

"Spread thy wings," they say unto me. "For He will awaken. He will terribly shake the earth."

**Excerpt from Résumé: Ms. Jennifer Langsam—
Donated by Mrs. Ardiss Langsam, Mother:**

OBJECTIVE: I am seeking part-time summer employment in an office or restaurant where I can draw on and develop my people skills. I am comfortable working with people of all ages. Working outdoors or with animals would be a plus.

ACKNOWLEDGMENTS

To Leslie Daniels, teacher, agent, and extraordinary friend, who believed in these stories before they existed, and to Amy Scheibe and Martha Levin of Free Press, who believed in them once they did.

To the Iowa Writers' Workshop, the Wisconsin Institute of Creative Writing at The University of Wisconsin–Madison, the Arthur Jerome Foundation, the Sewanee Writers' Conference, and the Helene Wurlitzer Foundation of New Mexico, for space, time, resources, wisdom, and invaluable support.

To Don Lee and visiting editor Amy Bloom of *Ploughshares,* Rob Spillman, Holly MacArthur, and Michelle Wildgen of *Tin House,* Sasha West of *Gulf Coast,* Ryan Bartelmay of *Columbia: A Journal of Literature and Art,* Lois Hauselman and Gina Frangello of *Other Voices,* and David Schuman of *The Land-Grant College Review,* for printing earlier versions of many of the stories appearing here.

To brilliant colleagues June Edelstein, Lisa Lerner, Jonathan Blum, Amber Dermont, Kathleen Hughes, Andrew Porter, Stephen Schottenfeld, Karen E. Bender, Sarah Schulman, Philip Pardi, John Valadez, Nancy Ann Chatty, John Martin, Gavin Carey, Richard Wofford, Matt Tyrnauer, Ashley Crow, Carole D'Andrea, Katherine Pettus, and Susan Kaufman, for their inspiration and first-rate guidance.

To beloved moviemaker, collaborator, and partner in crime

Eva Brzeski, co-creator of Apple Valley Productions and the feature film *Last Seen*, for one of the best adventures and friendships I've ever had.

To the families of Reinhorn, Schaefer, Putka, Cooper, and Wilson, for who they are and continue to be.

To The New Bozena, good coffee, and rock 'n' roll music, which goes without saying.

To Edison the dog, and Ada the horse, R.I.P.

And to my soul mate and partner, Rainn, for his inexplicable amazing-ness, and to our son, Walter McKenzie, whose story has only just begun.

About the Author

HOLIDAY REINHORN is a graduate of the Iowa Writers' Work-shop; a recipient of a Tobias Wolff Award, as well as a Carl Djerassi Fiction Fellowship from the University of Wisconsin–Madison; and a finalist for the PEN/Amazon.com Short Story Award. Her stories have appeared in *Tin House, Ploughshares, Columbia, Gulf Coast,* and other magazines. She lives in Los Angeles..